Valentine's Day TIGERS

THE HOLIDAY SHIFTER MATES
BOOK THREE

KESTRA PINGREE

Living in Fantasy

Valentine's Day Tigers
Text copyright © 2019 Kestra Pingree
kestrapingree.com

All rights reserved.

No part of this book may be used or reproduced in any manner whatsoever without written permission from the author except in the case of brief quotations embodied in critical articles or reviews. Any unauthorized reproduction or distribution of this copyrighted work is illegal.

This book is a work of fiction.

August 2019 edition
First digital publication: January 2019
First print publication: August 2018

Cover design by Kestra Pingree
Printed in the U.S.A.

ISBN-13: 9781087352084

10 9 8 7 6 5 4 3 2 1

CHAPTER 1

THE SOFT GLOW OF White Magic highlighted Yuri Lenkov's skin. It was time for another healing session with the White Witch named Josh. Lance Lenkov forgot how many times Josh had done this for his brother in just half a month. It felt a lot longer than that. The nerves that always followed Lance as he watched each session made everything slow down to an agonizing speed, like the moment would never end because he was always on high alert. At least Lance could say he was getting used to it. Time felt normal today. Things were just… quiet.

Yuri's skin looked warm and tan again, instead of

VALENTINE'S DAY TIGERS

the pale, clammy stretch of flesh it had become in December. Lance's skin was naturally void of any pigment; some gave him a hard time for it, claiming he looked diseased, but those people had no idea what they were talking about. They had never seen someone laid up in bed, sweat pouring down his skin like a river that would never run dry.

It was a new year. Lance hoped those sickly details were nothing but a distant memory now.

Josh had dark circles under his eyes these days. He looked otherwise healthy, but he was working tirelessly for the Lenkovs, and Lance didn't know how to feel about that. It was almost like the witch had voluntarily placed himself under house arrest because he never left. He had this driving need to prove he'd do everything in his power to help Yuri, to change the twins' minds on witches or some nonsense. Well, maybe it was working. This had become their daily routine, and Lance didn't see Josh as a threat anymore.

Lance had been going stir crazy, being stuck in small as fuck Eurio, Alaska, but he was resigned to it now. His brother came before anyone else.

Josh's glowing hands hovered over Yuri's forehead. Yuri lay flat on his back, hands on his stomach with his eyes closed. He looked peaceful enough, but he

2

wasn't sleeping. This vulnerable position was apparently the easiest way for Josh to do his witch healing thing.

The silence made Lance's mind wander.

He scrubbed a hand over his face. He was sporting dark circles under his eyes these days too, but he didn't know why he felt so tired when he wasn't the one with Black Magic nestled in his brain. It was all that worrying. Stress could kill a tiger shifter as easily as anyone else, he figured.

Also, it was extremely hard to function without a goal. There was no point in sitting at his computer to read medical theses anymore. He had spent hours upon hours doing that, trying to figure out the best way to help his brother, but he was never the one who was going to fix him. Josh was the only one, after all these years, who was getting any results, and that left Lance sitting uselessly at the bedside during these sessions.

Thankfully, Lance wasn't forced to sit around all day every day. Yuri had a new burst of energy this last week. That had preoccupied Lance more than enough—especially since he always had to divert Yuri from his bad habit of doing things that were way too questionable. Lance crushed Yuri's usual antics because it was too much too soon. Truthfully, Lance had

VALENTINE'S DAY TIGERS

never exactly loved Yuri's love for all things dangerous and often stupid anyway. He wouldn't be able to stop him forever, but it was what it was.

Yuri flinched. Lance grabbed his brother's hand and squeezed, doing whatever he could to reassure him of his presence. He also bit back the words he wanted to speak. Interrupting Josh wasn't a good thing, but Lance wanted to check in with Yuri every step of the way. Yuri told him it was too much. It probably was.

Yuri was likely getting restless too. This session had almost reached the hour mark. Lying still like this, without being physically laid up, was a real feat for Yuri.

Maybe Yuri was well enough for Lance to steal a little time for himself by taking a quick trip to Fairbanks. It was a small city, but humongous compared to Eurio. It was the place Lance turned to when he needed information, seeing as Eurio just recently conformed to using the internet like the rest of the world. Fairbanks also had a library. And, sometimes, Fairbanks was good for a change of pace, a place where Lance could get away from all the shifter stuff. It was like stepping into a different world and pretending to be someone else for a day. He never intended on meeting anyone there, though, but unexpected things tended to happen in life.

Lance wondered if Ash missed him. He wondered what they were doing. He wondered if they were still playing at Tipsy or if they had moved on and forgotten all about him. They should have. It was in their best interest, and it was likely all in his imagination that they had been flirting for the past few months.

His chest hurt at the thought.

You're being stupid, he told himself.

Yuri was the only one who mattered. He was the only one who ever mattered. Lance concentrated on his brother's face and the light cast by the witch's White Magic as if to remind himself of this fact. He had to look after his brother. Yuri needed him. This was his place.

"That's it for today," Josh said. "Ask Yuri how he's feeling." The magic flickered out like a candle that had been blown out. Josh reclaimed his hands as he slouched in the wooden chair that was supporting him. He was spent. He always was after administering to Yuri.

Lance stood up, intending to touch Yuri's shoulder, but Yuri sat up right before he did. Yuri almost smashed his forehead into Lance's nose. His eyes were wide and wild, and Lance immediately went on red

VALENTINE'S DAY TIGERS

alert.

"What's wrong?" Lance asked and hurriedly used his hands to say the same thing in American Sign Language.

"Say something else!" Yuri demanded.

"What? Why?"

A big grin overtook Yuri's face. Yuri had always been magnetic, bright, and alluring, but Lance hadn't seen him like *this* in a long time.

"I can *hear* you," Yuri said. He grabbed the back of Lance's neck and pulled him down. Lance almost squished him. He wouldn't have worried about that if Yuri hadn't seemed so fragile lately, but he was. So, he caught himself with his hands spread to either side of his brother on the mattress—despite Yuri applying an insane amount of pressure, as if he wanted Lance to smother him.

"I can understand you," Yuri said. "God, it's so good to hear your voice, really hear it. It's different than I remember."

Yuri held Lance close, acting like he was afraid he wouldn't be able to understand Lance if he was just a few inches farther away. Lance was too shocked to say much at first. It had been eight years since his brother could understand his words. His pure word deafness was gone? After all this time, it was gone? It had been this big, mysterious ailment, and it was just... gone?

Lance hugged his brother rather than speak. His throat tightened, and all he could do was grab the back of Yuri's neck in return and squeeze. He squeezed and squeezed, hoping he could transfer his relief.

Yuri roughly pushed him away after that. He slugged Lance's arm and grinned. He was feral, and he always would be, sick or not. Static seemed to jump off his skin. "Say something else," Yuri said.

"I can't think of anything to say." Lance choked back tears. God, he was such a mess lately. "I can't even understand what's going on. You can really hear me, understand me? Do you know how long it's been, Yuri?"

"For-fucking-ever."

Lance had forgotten all about Josh, but the witch was standing now, a smile on his face. He reached in his pocket for something: his cell phone. "I'll leave you two alone. I need to tell Cedar the good news."

The witch hurried out of the Lenkovs' room, but Lance called to him before he could disappear. "Josh, thank you."

Josh held on to the doorjamb as he looked over his shoulder and nodded. Then he was gone.

VALENTINE'S DAY TIGERS

"I wasn't holding my breath on this happening, but I was hoping," Yuri said. "PWD has been such a bitch."

Lance tried to laugh, but it turned into a choking sound. He couldn't escape it. Oh, he was happy, but there was a pit in his stomach. It grew and sunk. His stomach got heavier, and he couldn't stop this toxic thought from entering his mind: *Yuri doesn't need me anymore.* The burning in his eyes meant tears were about to follow. Lance had never been much of a crier in the past, but that had changed in December when he thought he would lose his brother forever.

"Hey, what's wrong?" Yuri asked. He wiped away a tear that rolled down Lance's cheek. "Stop. No crying."

Lance tried to say something back, but his throat was swollen. No words would come. He wanted to excuse the tears as a manifestation of his relief, but that was not true. If Yuri was cured, he didn't need Lance anymore.

Yuri had never needed Lance.

Lance had always followed in Yuri's footsteps like a shadow. He tried to keep up with his magnetic brother, but now he had to face the reality he could ignore when Yuri started having seizures. Yuri needed him then, and he needed him even more after the seizure that left him with PWD. Not anymore. Yuri hadn't had a seizure since Josh began working on him, and now he could communicate as well as anyone else. He would go out there, into the world. He'd find something, and he'd leave. He'd probably find a mate like Mateo, start his own family, and Lance would be alone because he would never have those things.

A horrible part of Lance's brain replayed words he wished he could forget: *"Don't lie. You don't love me."*

He rebuked the memory. *I didn't lie.*

He wiped away another tear that had escaped his eye and was finally able to speak. "I'm just happy."

"You've been doing way too much crying lately, bro," Yuri said. He wrestled Lance down so they lay side by side on the bed and kept his hand warm and firm on the back of Lance's neck as their foreheads connected. Lance grasped Yuri's arm like a lifeline, almost clawing into one of the many tattoos they had gotten together. Yuri was warm, his normal warm. Not too hot. Not sweating and sick.

"I'm really happy for you, Yuri. Really happy."

CHAPTER 2

EVERYONE WAS CALLED TO the Lodge for a meeting. Yuri went along with it because that was what everyone else was doing, and Lance told him to come. Since when did they start having meetings in the Lodge? Oh, right. Since Cedar became Gale's mate. That polar bear liked to put things in order. She liked to make everything a big to-do for the entire town. It wasn't even anything important. Today she was talking about Valentine's Day, which was just over a week away.

"So, I'm thinking we could make chocolates and cards here at the Lodge. Then, on Valentine's Day, we'll decorate the Lodge and have the dance," Cedar said.

She sat at the front of the Lodge, her chair against the wall, and held Gale's big hand. Both hands rested atop one of her plentiful thighs. She seemed to always have a smile on her plump lips. She also did all the talking these days.

Yuri figured Cedar was the one who officially ran the town now, even though she wasn't titled one of Eurio's Alphas. Those spots belonged to Gale and Weston, who both seemed happy to let Cedar keep going. Actually, they looked distracted. Gale was busy staring at Cedar with this dopey smile on his face, and Weston wasn't fairing much better with his mate, Cary. They sat where everyone could see them, and they couldn't be bothered to look out at their small crowd.

Yuri wondered if they'd ever look away. It was like an eternity of them staring at each other. Their eyes couldn't be that interesting because they were just *eyes*, the same as anyone else's.

"Let's do it!" some shifter said. Yuri didn't recognize her. She was new. Eurio recently received a bunch of new shifters from Trinity, the biggest damn shifter alliance in the world and Josh's employer. Many of them were young and newly mated, feeding Cedar's apparent obsession with romance. It also meant making eyes, making eyes *everywhere*.

VALENTINE'S DAY TIGERS

Yuri sunk deeper into the bench he was seated on, his back resting against the table behind him. He folded his arms and resisted the urge to roll his eyes. The chocolate sounded tasty, and he wouldn't mind finding a free female to take to bed after the dance, but that was about it. It had been way too long since he had had good sex—which sparked a thought.

Yuri turned to Lance and whispered, "Let's blow this joint and go to a bar."

"You've been going nonstop since your PWD went away," Lance said. "Slow down a little. We just went to a bar."

"I have. We've been scoping out all the small fries while I've been getting back on my feet. It's all been practice for Fairbanks, which we haven't gotten to yet. We're going to Tipsy. There are way more people there. Tonight we're gonna get laid. You know how much easier it is to get laid when you can carry a conversation like a normal person?"

Lance stiffened and sat up board straight. "Can we do something else or go to a different bar? I don't like Tipsy."

"When have you been to Tipsy? You go to bars on your own, Lance? All those times you've been in Fairbanks for the 'library'? You would have had to have

12

gone on your own because I've never been. We crashed a lot of places together when we were sixteen, but not bars, and we haven't been to Fairbanks a lot since PWD hit. You'd never let me drink because of the seizures and shit. Now that I've been miraculously healed for, what, half a month, I need to make up for lost time."

"It was for your own good. I didn't want you to get worse because of something as stupid as alcohol. Bars suck anyway. Let's do something else."

Lance was being vague as usual. For some reason, he didn't want to answer Yuri's questions.

"Lenkovs, you listening?" Cedar called. "I've still been talking for the last five minutes. You know, about our plans. Do you know what days we're doing things? The chocolates? Even if you don't have a mate, it's always nice to give chocolates to those you love and appreciate. I promise they'll be delicious."

"Yeah, whatever. You'll tell us again. You make sure you get heard one way or another," Yuri said.

Cedar folded her arms and tilted her head down to give him a dissatisfied look. Gale pursed his lips. Cedar hadn't been in Eurio that long, so she didn't know Yuri the way those who had been here for years did. But she was learning quickly. His personality sort of clashed with hers since she was all structure and he was

VALENTINE'S DAY TIGERS

structureless.

"This is boring, and I'm leaving," Yuri said and stood up. He glanced at his other side, where Mateo and his mate were sitting. Mateo looked up at him, but Austin did his whole avoiding-eye-contact thing. Typical.

"You're a bigger pain in the ass now than you ever were," Mateo said, but he was grinning.

"I'd invite you to come along, but you've got a mate holding you down. Imagine all the trouble you're missing out on. We used to go hard."

Mateo pulled Austin into him, just a little closer, likely to reassure him of his love—or some shit like that. Then Mateo turned to Lance like he was expecting him to say something on Yuri's behalf. Lance held Mateo's gaze with a neutral expression, giving nothing away. Well, other than Lance's neutral expression was as cold as all the snow and ice outside. He didn't use to look at Mateo like that.

Yuri shrugged. "No offense, Austin. You're boring, but if you're happy, that's what counts." He clapped Mateo on the shoulder. "If you ever want to get out and cause some trouble, you know who to get."

Yuri ignored the eyes following him as he exited the Lodge. He didn't bother waiting for Lance because

14

he knew he would follow. He threw his shoulders back and cracked his neck as whispers broke out.

"Should we stop him?" Cedar asked.

"No, he's fine," Gale said. "You didn't know him before his PWD, but this is pretty normal."

"Has he always been so flippant?"

"Yes. Believe it or not, he can be quite a smooth talker too. He didn't mean anything by it. It's that bold and nonchalant attitude that gets him so many eyes, for better or for worse." Then Gale shouted, "Did I say you could use one of our SUVs to go to Fairbanks?"

"I'll hot-wire one if you deny me the privilege," Yuri said without turning his head; Gale could hear him perfectly well.

"Maybe you should start thinking about the future, Yuri. What are your goals? You can't just mess around forever."

"What else are you supposed to do with your life?" Yuri tossed his hand back in a lazy goodbye and exited the building. He didn't bother shutting the door because, like clockwork, Lance was behind him, and he took care of it.

Satisfied, Yuri slung his arm over his brother's shoulders. "Tonight is going to be good."

Lance didn't have anything to say about that.

CHAPTER 3

THE SMALL STAGE WAS lit, and all the bleary-eyed patrons of the bar were at half-attention. Ash Nobody stood on that stage. Places like these were perfect for them to perform. No one came for Ash specifically because they never planned ahead. Ash was like a leaf carried on the wind; they went wherever it took them. Their social media following could try to keep up, but it wasn't easy. Ash liked it that way. They liked to drift into their own little world of music.

Together with their ukulele, Ash created a sanctuary no malevolent force could touch.

"This next song is very special to me," Ash told the audience as they pulled the microphone to their lips.

"You know how people say when you have a crush or love someone it feels like butterflies in your stomach? I never got what that meant, but I never got love either. It's an abstract concept, right? It's something only butterflies know. Or it was. After twenty-three years of being alive on this planet, I can say I'm in on the secret."

Ash took a moment to take in the crowd, to see this reality. It didn't look like much. The bright lights did an excellent job of concealing faces. It didn't matter anyway. Lance wasn't here again.

Once Ash strummed that first chord on the ukulele, setting the key for themself, all those ghostly silhouettes disappeared. It was just Ash and the music.

"'Something Only Butterflies Know,' everybody," Ash said, and then they sang for the one who wasn't there.

Walking along a road that never ends
A rhythm made by feet on earth
Lyrics and stories stream in my head
A record of all the places I've been
No destination made for me
I am on the road to nothing
And I meant to keep it at nothing
But a kaleidoscope of butterflies find me

VALENTINE'S DAY TIGERS

I have heard it said a time or two
There's something only butterflies know
It's a feeling, a wondrous feeling
It starts in your stomach and grows
No destination made for me
I am on the road to nothing
And I meant to keep it at nothing
But a kaleidoscope of butterflies find me

They fly from above
In a vortex called love
I swallow them whole
Then lose all control

It all starts with a look
A simple look from a stranger
A short exchange of words
There isn't any danger
Your eyes tell a story I've never heard
I hardly know you, but something inside of me stirs
That should be the end
I've recorded your story
But I come again
Guided by fluttering wings
Because your eyes tell a story I've never heard

What was cold is now warm, and there is more

That's when I know
I've discovered what only butterflies know

Ash kept their gaze soft and low to the ground, resting on the synthetic fur of their boots when they strummed the last chord. This was the only love song Ash had written. Maybe. Ash didn't know if it was a love song or not, but it was born of love, dedicated to a special someone they had bonded with, the same someone they hadn't seen in over a month: Lance.

Clapping filled the bar and drew Ash out of their isolation. Ash had never felt so empty. They had always been detached from everything because life taught them to be. Life turned them into a nomad, and it was time to move again. Lance wasn't coming back, and Ash would carry their first broken heart.

Ash stepped down from the stage as several people made comments and offered drinks. Ash ignored every one of them because they were leaving. They were going back to the Campfire Hotel. They'd play some more music and get lost for a while. Then they'd pack up and leave. Tonight Ash couldn't even bring themself to take a picture for their Instagram followers. It would have

VALENTINE'S DAY TIGERS

been simple enough, a quick smile and a selfie, but Ash didn't feel like smiling, not even for a second. They kept swallowing like they were trying to keep something from crawling up their throat. Their vision shimmered, and it wasn't because of the bright lights that had pierced their eyes onstage.

After weaving their way through the last of the tables, Ash would have had a clear shot to the door if not for the man who blocked their way. Ash stopped and reluctantly raised their chin to get a look at the guy. Their eyes had to scale a wall of muscle before reaching a million-watt smile shining through a scruffy beard. The beard was only a few inches long, but it was thick, and it hid the finer features of the lower half of his face. His eyes were brown at a glance, but there was a subtle burst of orange somewhere deep inside of them; they resembled fire. Ash had been here, playing at Tipsy almost every night, for months now, but they had never seen this man before.

If Ash hadn't been heartbroken over Lance, they would have been more than intrigued by this newcomer; he was hot as fuck.

"You have the voice of an angel," he said. "Never met a gal who could sing like that."

"They and them," Ash said.

"What?" The man raised an eyebrow so subtly it was more of a visual cue than a reaction.

Ash held out their hand for him to shake. "Those are the pronouns I use."

The man took their hand. "Got it. I'm Yuri. What's your name?"

Ash liked that he didn't ask for an explanation. "My name's Ash. You would've heard that if you had been here when I started my session."

"Guilty. I almost missed your performance entirely, but I'm glad I didn't."

He was still holding Ash's hand and quickly ran his thumb across their knuckles before withdrawing. This guy was smooth. Brokenhearted or not, that one touch brought Ash's body to attention. This warm buzz flooded their skin, promising the sweet caress of distraction. That grin hadn't left Yuri's face. He was too endearing. Maybe the buzz Ash felt wasn't coming from inside of them at all. Maybe Ash's skin was catching invisible fireworks from Yuri. Maybe everyone in the room was because he was drawing many more eyes than Ash's. There were several salivating women and some salivating men who would have loved to steal his attention away.

"Are you a model?" Ash asked.

VALENTINE'S DAY TIGERS

"Hell no. That life wouldn't suit me. I'm a shower-and-go kind of guy."

"You're right. You look too rugged for that, but damn."

Yuri chuckled. It was a big sound that entered Ash's ears and sank all the way down to their core.

Suddenly Ash was smiling, too. Yuri's emotions were contagious. Ash had met similar people on their endless journey, but none of them were quite as magnetic. It was a bit unnerving. No, that wasn't it. There was nothing "wrong" with Yuri. It was the name: Yuri. Lance had told Ash that name before. Hearing it now, from this stranger, sent a pang through their chest that made them feel emptier. It was the kind of loneliness a single tree must have felt in the middle of a concrete city.

Yuri was the name of Lance's twin brother. Ash didn't know much beyond that since Lance was best described as a block of ice—when they first met him, anyway. Ash had to chip away at him to discover the warmth that hid at his center, but there was still plenty they didn't know and would never know. This couldn't be Lance's Yuri. Yeah, their skin tone and hair color were drastically different, but most importantly,

Lance's Yuri was very sick. This guy was a shining beacon of health.

"Can I buy you a drink?" Yuri asked.

"Maybe," Ash said.

"Or we can skip all the pussyfooting and start a fire somewhere." There was a glint in his eyes that danced like a flame. Ash decided his spirit was made of an indomitable fire. That was why they could see it in his eyes.

Ash hummed. They coyly stepped back from the stranger and made their way to the bar. They took an empty stool on the end and watched out of the corner of their eye as Yuri took a seat beside them.

"Warm honey-lemon water if you please, Frank," Ash said when the bartender came around.

"Already got you covered, kid," the old man said as he slid a mug their way.

"Thanks."

"What about you, boy?" Frank turned his attention to Yuri. "Damn, got enough muscle on you? You some kind of bodybuilder?" Ash couldn't blame Frank. Yuri was wearing a skintight t-shirt; it was impossible not to notice his physique and the tattoos emblazoned on his arms.

"Yes," Yuri deadpanned and put money on the

VALENTINE'S DAY TIGERS

counter. "Whiskey neat."

Frank set a shot glass down and poured the drink. When he slid it over to Yuri, Yuri knocked it back quick and tapped the glass back down on the counter. He showed his teeth and growled. "Give me another one, old man."

Frank did as he was asked and left to take care of another customer.

"So, what's this about starting fires?" Ash asked. "Were you joking?"

Yuri knocked back the next shot and hissed. "No joke, but it's probably illegal."

"Are you the dangerous sort?"

"If that's what you want me to be."

"You're just trying to appeal to my type?"

Yuri shrugged. His smile was playful. "I guess you could call me the dangerous sort, but don't knock it till you try it. Arson can be an interesting pastime. And tonight feels like a good night to make 'bad decisions.'" He made air quotes with his fingers.

"I don't think I've ever met anyone like you before, Yuri. Are you trying to get laid or are you looking for a partner in crime? I'm getting mixed messages."

"Yeah, I'm out of practice. Arson isn't usually a good pick-up line. What I'd really like is to fuck you, and however we get around to doing that is fine with me."

"What if I say no?"

"Then that's that. At least I put myself out there. Never any harm in doing that." His smile was so easy. Ash would have never described a smile as lazy before, but Yuri's was just that.

Ash laughed. Yuri probably had a few screws loose, but others had accused Ash of that same thing. Yuri looked like someone who could make them feel good, and Ash had no problems with breaking rules. Tonight, they'd welcome both things wholeheartedly. Alcohol could numb their feelings, music could take them away from this reality for a while, but maybe Yuri could do more.

Just then, the bar door slammed shut. The windows rattled with the force of it, drawing every eye in the bar, but there was nothing to see. The culprit was gone. Out a window, Ash saw a silhouette of someone hunched over, drawing up their coat collar to protect them from the snow as they slunk away. Someone was having a bad night. *Me too, person,* Ash thought. But maybe Ash's night was about to get a lot better. Or worse. That was also a possibility.

"Am I wrong in assuming you're a little wild?" Yuri

VALENTINE'S DAY TIGERS

asked. "Because if you're actually the careful type, we can stop this right now. I'm looking for someone who's reckless. I'm not offering dinner dates or anything romantic. I can't get the image of us fucking in a burning building out of my head." He moved in closer, and Ash stayed in place, firm as a statue. Their noses almost touched. "Dangerous and sexy," Yuri promised. "You in or out?"

"I've never had anyone offer something so outrageous, and I think you're serious about it."

Yuri tapped his fingers smoothly against the counter. It wasn't a twitch or a nervous action. It was calculating, a constant rhythm like the flick of a cat's tail. He was getting ready to pounce.

"I'm in," Ash said.

"You're either really dumb or you have no sense of self-preservation," Yuri remarked. "I fucked up with the whole fire thing almost right when I started talking to you. That's not how you pick up chicks, but you're different. So, I decided to roll with it to see what your reaction would be. I expected you to turn tail, but you're still here."

"The latter," Ash said. "It takes one to know one. I've done my fair share of reckless things, and I've got nothing to lose."

That brought out the gleam in Yuri's eyes tenfold, and it was followed by a big shit-eating grin. "When you could die tomorrow, why play it safe?"

Yuri's words were an odd echo in Ash's head. Ash went with the flow. The thought of dying tomorrow didn't scare them. They had thought about ending it all before, but they kept finding things that kept them going. Ash was hanging on to a narrow ledge. Sometimes, the ledge would start to crumble. Other times, it would hold steady as a mountain. Lance had almost given them the strength to climb up and leave the ledge behind forever, but then he disappeared without a word. Now the ledge was crumbling faster than ever. Ash was holding on to paper and it was tearing, unable to hold their weight.

Lance wasn't coming back, and Ash would fight through a broken heart. They wished the butterflies had kept their secret. It would have spared them this pain.

"Sounds like we're both people with nothing to lose," Ash said, "so let's play with fire."

CHAPTER 4

"**H**OW MUCH FARTHER, AND where are we going exactly?" Ash asked. "I'm starting to think you're a serial killer who wants to find the perfect place to bury my body."

"We're almost there, and I'm very offended," Yuri said. He scanned the snowy scenery outside the moving truck. If Yuri hadn't been a tiger shifter, he wouldn't have been able to see what he was looking for, but, as things stood, the dark wasn't much of a visual obstacle for him. "I remember I saw an abandoned building around here. We'll more likely be able to play the game if we're not in such a populated area."

"We're in the middle of nowhere officially now,"

Ash said.

"There." Yuri rolled down the window and pointed. "Park in that clearing over there, but don't go too far out."

"Wow, it's like all the trees disappear over there, huh? I wonder why."

Ash turned their ancient truck off the road. Yuri wasn't exaggerating with that assessment. The truck was like an old man with blotchy, saggy skin, but it was well-suited for this kind of weather, rugged and ready to go on any kind of adventure. If Yuri had been in a different mood, and if it hadn't been so dark out for a human, he might have suggested an off-road adventure that could have ended with sex in the truck.

Ash was hot. Fucking hot. Yuri was half-hard right now. He couldn't get the memory of their perfect tits out of his head. They had worn nothing but a tank top back at Tipsy. The material was thin, and Ash wasn't wearing a bra. It left little to the imagination. Their boobs were the perfect size to palm and knead. And their thighs. Ash's thighs were thick and strong; it was obvious they had spent a lot of time on their feet. They didn't wear makeup, and they didn't need to. Their dark brown skin was unblemished, and their eyelashes were full and black. Their look would have been all

VALENTINE'S DAY TIGERS

natural if not for their curly bleached-white hair and the faded rainbow coloring the right half of it.

Oh yeah, Yuri was ready to get laid—after they fucked up some shit.

"All right, let's get out," Yuri said when Ash had parked and the snow had stopped screaming. "Good job not driving us into the ice. We'd be swimming right now."

"Ice? What the hell?"

"It's a lake."

"You might have mentioned that before."

"Details."

"I didn't even know there was a lake out here." Ash squinted.

Yuri chuckled. "Doesn't matter. I would've told you before we drove into it. Promise."

Ash turned off the headlights. "So, are we on the wrong side? I don't see any abandoned buildings."

"There's one across the lake, but we're on the right side." Yuri pointed again, now that Ash's fragile human eyes wouldn't be competing with the truck's headlights.

"Oh, I see it. I think."

Yuri winked and kicked open his door. He stepped out into the snow, looked at the trees behind

30

him, and back out at the iced-over lake. He tugged at the collar of his coat as the cold penetrated his uncovered skin. What could he do to make this as exhilarating as possible? Well, he was stuck on the image of fire, so running with that sounded like a good idea. First, they'd need some branches to act as torches. Fire wouldn't start too easily in this weather, but there was a gas can in the truck bed, and Yuri was willing to bet it wasn't empty.

Ash didn't question him. They waited patiently, silently observing. It was refreshing. He usually resorted to doing shit like this by himself since everyone else started complaining about the situations he'd get them into. "It's too dangerous, Yuri," they'd say and, "You need to rest, Yuri." Lance and Mateo never nagged so much until his seizures got worse and worse. They didn't get it. They never had. He was in it for the thrill, and for the novelty. It was a chance to live and to remind himself that he was alive.

To conquer death.

Ash followed Yuri as he made his way to the trees. He shook the snow off branches to get a better look at them and eventually settled for snapping off a couple. He shredded them bit by bit, stripping protruding

VALENTINE'S DAY TIGERS

twigs and adjusting their height until they were virtually the same.

"Damn," Ash said. "I know you're wearing gloves, but you practically did that with your bare hands. Are you some kind of lumberjack, then?"

"Close enough. I've done it before."

"Maybe a sculptor of some sort."

Yuri shook his head and chuckled.

Ash tried again. "Jack of all trades."

"Probably the closest you'll get to pinning me down, sexy—and by that, I mean good luck."

"Give me a hint. Or maybe danger is the thing that defines you, just like music defines me."

"Decent assessment."

"Do you usually play hard to get?"

"Uh, yeah. Usually works out the best for me."

Ash shook their head, but the corners of their lips upturned into the first smile Yuri had seen.

Yuri held the almost-torches in his hands as he led the way back to the truck bed. He set the branches down and started digging underneath the tarp.

"Help yourself. What's mine is yours," Ash said. Yuri might have interpreted that as a warning laced in sarcasm, but there was a teasing tone to Ash's angelic voice. Oh, Yuri was enjoying this one. All the chicks he

3 2

had fucked in the past were way too uptight. He never got to do anything beyond straight sex with them. Which was fine. He enjoyed it, but this was already proving to be far more entertaining. He and Ash could probably be friends.

There was no need for further invitation. Ash told Yuri to help himself, so he did. He ripped up some threadbare blankets he found underneath the tarp and wrapped strips around one end of the branches. Now they looked like proper torches. It felt like they were going on some medieval campaign. Maybe they'd slay a dragon. As if those existed. But hell, who was to say they didn't? Yuri was a tiger shifter, and most humans were ignorant of his existence. Dragons could be like chameleons, blending into everything, more hidden than any shifter or witch.

What a thought.

Yuri picked up the gas can and was pleased to hear liquid sloshing inside. He held it out to Ash. "Want to do the honors?"

Ash shivered. "You're sure nobody's in that building, right?"

"Trust me, when you get close to it, you'll know. It's an old boathouse with the roof caved in. It's barely standing. We're not going to hurt anybody. That's not

VALENTINE'S DAY TIGERS

my thing."

Ash studied him for a moment, green eyes catching on moonlight, and then nodded. "Good to know." Yuri focused on the sound of their heartbeat, waiting for any inconsistencies, but it was as calm as the iced-over lake. Ash wasn't afraid. They weren't even excited. Yuri needed to change that last part. This was about getting an adrenaline rush.

With an easy sweep of his hand, Yuri claimed the torches and held them out over the snow. He nodded toward them, inviting Ash to drench them. It didn't take much more than that. Ash grabbed the gas can and gingerly tipped it over, soaking the fabric-encased tips. They were careful about not being too gasoline-happy, but they didn't hold back either.

"You've got matches in the glovebox, don't you?" Yuri asked. He was pretty sure he glimpsed a box in there earlier.

"Yep," Ash said.

"Man, you have weird shit everywhere. I like it."

Ash snorted, but they smiled again, bigger than last time. They moved their hand over their heart and pressed down on their puffy coat. Then they gave an elaborate bow. "Thank you, kind sir."

God, Ash was weird. In a good way.

"Okay, the goal," Yuri said. "We race across the lake with these torches lit and burn down the boathouse."

"That's it?" Ash asked incredulously.

"Naked. We're doing this naked."

"Not sure how sex is going to work into this. I was planning on sex, Yuri."

"If you're turned on by the time we get to the boathouse and set it on fire, that'll be my new type."

It would be miserably cold enough for Yuri to run naked out here in his human skin, but Ash was *human*. They'd freeze their perfect tits off in this weather. Yuri expected Ash to back out at this point. This was not the way to get laid, but hell if he wasn't turned on right now. He didn't know why he was pushing so hard, though. There was something about Ash that just kept gnawing at him. The dark depths of Ash's eyes made him want to push more and more.

This whole situation would have been like pulling teeth with Lance—except it wouldn't have included any of the kinky shit of course. He could hear his brother now: "You want hypothermia after you're finally all better?" Why, yes. Yes, he did.

"Okay," Ash said. "Let's do it."

"Let's do it?" Yuri echoed. He measured Ash with

VALENTINE'S DAY TIGERS

a hard look. They didn't flinch, and their heartbeat was steady and calm. The haunting tone of their voice sounded in his ears as he remembered the song they sang back at Tipsy. That was the voice of someone who was lost and begging for answers. Ash would go along with anything. A wild grin overtook Yuri's face, and the first drop of adrenaline hit his system.

"That's what I said," Ash challenged. They opened the truck's passenger door and pulled out the box of matches.

Yuri smirked. "Did I ever pick the right one tonight."

After setting the matches on the end of the truck bed, Ash unzipped their coat. Yuri would have liked to stand by and watch, but that wouldn't have been fair. This was a different kind of strip show. It wasn't the sexiest or easiest thing to do with all those winter layers either. It would have been ideal if the boots could come off last, but it was impossible to slip off pants with those clunkers. The cold sunk into the soles of Yuri's bare feet, and he doubled his speed, yanking off his pants and boxers at the same time. Then he looked up at Ash and got the breath knocked out of his lungs.

Everything about Ash was sexy, starting with that crazy rainbow hair and ending all the way down to their toes sinking into the snow. Yuri only glimpsed the slight curve of their stomach before they turned around and gave him a perfect view of their backside. That ass was everything: plump, round, and firm. Yuri was so hot, he barely felt the cold now.

Ash lit a match, and Yuri tamped down the need building inside of him as he grabbed the torches. When Ash turned to face him again, his nose was hit with a wave of sweet arousal. Ash was just as turned on as he was. They held out the match, waiting for Yuri to reciprocate with the torches, but they let their eyes wander his body at the same time. Since their flesh was showing goosebumps, Yuri didn't let the moment last. He held the torches together, and Ash lit them up.

Yuri was going to get laid tonight.

The two of them exchanged looks and shouted in unison, "Go!"

They shot off as best they could with the snow grabbing their feet each time they touched down. It took a few seconds to gain momentum, and then they were sliding on ice. Yuri was in the lead, but he was happy to adjust his pace to Ash's; it was a subtle change Ash wouldn't notice. The ice should have been plenty thick, but one never knew. As if to prove that point, Yuri ended up finding a thin patch. It cracked under his

VALENTINE'S DAY TIGERS

weight, threatening to trap him under freezing waters. But he was agile. Thanks to his tiger, the slippery surface couldn't best him.

With a well-placed kick, the ice shattered underneath Yuri, and he took to the air. He touched down on thick ice and slid forward, but he held himself up with ease. The fire from his torch burned strong.

"Careful over there. You'll lose if your flame goes out." Ash called. They dipped forward when they hit a bit of craggy ice, but they caught themself.

Yuri chuckled. "Back at you, Ash."

They pressed forward. Their torches slightly staved off the cold as they continued to burn bright, but that aching numbness was starting to set into Yuri's extremities. It was eating its way down to Yuri's bones. That meant Ash was feeling it much worse. Yuri glanced back at them, but they hadn't slowed. Their eyes were trained on that boathouse. Silent determination and buzzing adrenaline would see them through. The ice could crack underneath them at any second, but they kept pushing. Yuri's heart hammered in his chest, and another burst of energy shot through his system. He could overcome anything.

This was what it meant to be alive.

Yuri looked over his shoulder again when he

heard Ash's heart beating in time with his, and just when he was starting to think that their heart might be unmovable. This was good. This kind of thrill, sharing this desire to conquer, to face danger and defeat it, was something he had only really shared with Lance because of all they had been through together growing up. Mateo had touched the surface, and Lance protested when things went "too far." But Ash was different. They could keep up.

Yuri dug in his feet to slide across the last little stretch of ice and hit snowy, but solid, ground first. He almost tripped, but he caught himself. His torch was alight, but it was burning down quickly. And then Ash was at his side. Their skin was smooth, absent of goosebumps, but they'd freeze as solid as a block of ice as soon as the adrenaline left their system. Ash flicked him a look, and then they both went inside of the dilapidated building and started setting the driest spaces on fire.

Without gasoline to spark the flames, it was much harder to get a fire started here with all the cold and wet wood, but there were a few dry places that eventually accepted the flames. And those flames grew. They heated up the entire building, canceling out the ice bit by bit as the fire spread.

VALENTINE'S DAY TIGERS

Ash and Yuri dropped their torches into the burning pit as the building creaked around them, but they stayed inside. They looked up through the burning beams and out into the smoke-obscured night sky. The stars randomly peeked through like twinkling Christmas lights.

Ash flung their arms out to either side of them, threw back their head, and started laughing. Light shone in their eyes. Maybe it could have been written off as a reflection of the fire, but Yuri knew it was more than that. Ash was alive. Really alive. This wasn't the same Ash he had taken out, the one who had nothing to lose. Now they were feeling. Furious. Triumphant. Their lips were blue, but the cold didn't matter.

They were alive.

CHAPTER 5

Y URI COULDN'T WAIT ANYMORE. He stepped up, grabbed Ash by the waist, and captured their lips with his. He kissed the cold away, sharing his body heat. Ash was right there with him. They groped his ass, encouraging him to keep going. Ash tasted good, sweet like honey, but their taste also burned. When their tongues touched, little explosions set off in Yuri's mouth like those candy rocks kids adored.

A decrepit wooden beam fell to Yuri's right. It sizzled and then burst. Pieces flew in the air and burrowed into skin. Ash and Yuri flinched, but neither one of them stopped. They clung to each other, and

VALENTINE'S DAY TIGERS

soon their bodies were good and hot.

"You better not care about condoms," Yuri said, breathing heavily into Ash's mouth, "because I don't have any. Left them in the truck."

"I'm surprised you even thought about condoms," Ash said. "I thought it was a good night to make 'bad decisions.' Also, I doubt you've had sex with many if these are your baseline requirements."

That made Yuri laugh. "You're the first I've ever done this with, Ash. That's not the reason why I haven't had more sex, though. Not that it matters."

Another beam fell and more bits of burning, broken wood flung into the air. It was hot and punishing. Ash whimpered, but Yuri devoured their mouth as the fire burned brighter. Ash made delicious sounds, even as he swallowed them whole, and he couldn't get enough. He was hard as hard and wanted to take them now, but they'd burn up if they stayed in here too much longer.

He unlocked their lips and guided Ash out of the burning boathouse. The snow outside was melting. They went a "safe" distance away, where the snow stayed cold. It soothed and clawed at Yuri's burns at the same time. He embraced it and pinned Ash to the ground. Ash arched their back in reaction to the snow nipping at their backside, bumping their body into his. They grabbed the back of his neck, fingers pressing like daggers into his skin.

"Let's do it," Ash said.

"Gladly," Yuri replied.

He was about to dive back in, but Ash grabbed his right bicep and squeezed. He paused. Ash was fixated on one of his tattoos. It was the one on his right shoulder, a Siberian tiger's face. He shared this one with his brother. Everything was the same except for the colors. Yuri's was orange with sunburst eyes like his tiger, while Lance's was white with ice-blue eyes for the same reason.

"What?" Yuri asked. "Please tell me you aren't done."

"I swear I've seen this tattoo before," Ash said. The look in their eyes made it seem like they were a million miles away all of a sudden. But then their eyes caught fire again, and they pulled Yuri on top of them. "How are you so warm?"

Yuri's answer was to kiss Ash silent. They were like two animals fighting, biting, and clawing. He had Ash pinned pretty well, but they managed to get their hands in between them and raked their nails down his abdomen. Then they grabbed his thick length, running

VALENTINE'S DAY TIGERS

their hands down to the sensitive head and stealing his breath away. Yuri grabbed Ash's thigh and continued to move his hand slowly until he cupped their sex. Ash's skin burned red as they puffed out breaths of hot air into the cold. Yuri coated his fingers with their slick heat and then pushed two inside of them. He wasted no time pumping fast and hard. They were a tangle of limbs until Ash lost all of their strength as he made them come violently. They let out a mangled scream. And then their strength was back. Ash yanked down on the back of Yuri's neck, pancaking their bodies, and then they rolled over. Ash was on top now.

Ash held themself up with their knees to either side of Yuri. "Get up," they said, and Yuri was happy to oblige.

Yuri grunted as Ash squeezed his balls, forceful, and yet gentle enough not to hurt. Then Ash sunk down, positioning themself between his legs, and swallowed him whole and all the way down their throat with that one motion. Yuri nearly died. The constriction Ash managed was perfect. Yuri had to grab their short hair and use every bit of strength he had not to pull it out as he trembled. Ash took him in and out quickly. No one had ever given him a blowjob like this.

Just when Yuri was sure Ash would swallow him

whole again, and he would blow, Ash grabbed his hips. He was so unsteady, it was enough to make him fall to his back. Snow sunk into his skin and burned like salt in a wound, but he quickly forgot about that. Ash grabbed his dick and sat down on his hips. Yuri pierced Ash as they sunk lower and lower, and then Ash rode him with a ferocity he had never experienced. He sat up as far as he could, supporting himself with an arm and gripping Ash with the other. He screamed when Ash came crashing down around him, and the tension in his body crested. Wave after wave he came, and Ash moved. Yuri rocked his hips up in time to meet them until they were totally spent. His hot cum leaked down and out, coating them both as it cooled hard and sticky. They stayed connected like that while they caught their breath.

The boathouse had been reduced to a smoldering mass. Smoke was dense overhead, but an aurora was showing face, a bright green band of moving lights in the night. It bathed Ash's skin in a color that didn't belong to this world. It fit the wild colors of their hair. Hell, they were sexy, leaning into him with every shuddering breath they took. Yuri wanted to go another round, but a high-pitched wail echoed in the distance.

Sirens.

VALENTINE'S DAY TIGERS

"Ah, fuck," he said. "That's our cue."

Ash winced as they struggled to their feet. Their legs were shaky, and Yuri understood. He wasn't feeling much steadier at the moment. Also, he was getting hard again. He would have been down to run several more rounds with Ash like this because this was *good* sex.

"Time to go." Yuri held out his hand. Ash took it with their shaking hand, and Yuri pulled them close. He swept them off their feet and carried them in his arms as he made his way back across the lake with a grace and poise only a big-cat shifter like himself could have. Ash was too blissed out to notice the difference and settled for clinging to him, trusting him to get them to safety. Ash's body temperature was about to reach frostbite-cold, but Yuri got them back to the truck before it could become anything serious.

He searched through Ash's clothes for the keys and started the engine. Then he turned on the heat and wrapped Ash in a blanket they kept in the backseat. They had a pillow back there too. Yuri wondered how many nights Ash had spent alone in this old truck.

The sirens were getting louder, so Yuri forced on his pants and took the driver's seat. Red and blue lights pierced the night as Yuri backed up and then continued

46

off-road into the trees. Ash pulled the blanket closer around them and didn't say a word. They simply watched, and Yuri let the silence stay. It didn't feel awkward or stiff. A residual high made the moment full.

When Yuri was satisfied they had gotten far enough away, he parked the truck near black and white spruces. They were far from the road, and no one would think to look for them in here. The police would probably never find their tracks since they were clear on the other side of the lake from the boathouse—and ice didn't leave good tracks. They were much closer to Eurio than they were to Fairbanks now, so Yuri figured he'd run the rest of the way home in his tiger form. However, he wanted to bring back his clothes, so he looked for a spare bag Ash was almost guaranteed to have lying around somewhere in the truck.

"I've never done anything like that before," Ash said at last. "Thanks. It was… exhilarating."

"Sure," Yuri replied. Ash didn't call him out on rummaging through their things, so he kept going.

"You should come by the bar again."

"Why? You want to do this again?"

Ash shrugged. "Why not? And maybe we'll actually have a normal conversation over some drinks next

VALENTINE'S DAY TIGERS

time. I think I'd like to get to know you better."

"All right, but not if you want to get to know me better for potential boyfriend material. I don't do dates, and I don't do romance. Friends and fuck-buddies are it."

Ash laughed. "Yeah, that's all I meant. Friends. I'm not looking for a partner. I'm currently recovering from a broken heart, I think. On second thought, don't bother. I'll be moving on before long. It was nice to meet you, though, Yuri." They wrapped the blanket tighter around them and stared out the window. The void was back in their eyes. Where had the light gone?

"Fuck that," Yuri said. "What did you do tonight?"

"Something crazy and stupid?"

"You beat fire."

Ash's heart rate sped up as if they were recalling the memory. Light shimmered in their eyes for an instant. "Yeah, I did."

"Fuck everyone else and everything else. You got out alive. If you can do that, you can do anything. Nobody can take that away from you."

Ash tore their gaze from the window to look at Yuri. "You know, I was ready to give up today. But now... now I feel different."

Yuri nodded. "Make the most of every moment,

Ash. You never know when it's going to end. Might as well enjoy it while you can." He grabbed a couple of old plastic shopping bags he found wedged in between the cushion and the backrest of the backseat and then opened his door.

"What are you doing?"

"I'm going home. It's not too far from here. Also, I'm taking these bags."

Ash's mouth dropped open as if they wanted to say something, but they shook their head instead.

"You good to find your way back to Fairbanks?" Yuri asked.

"I'll just back up until I can turn around and follow our trail back. It hasn't snowed, so the tracks will be easy enough to see."

"You might want to put on your clothes before you do that."

"Worried about me?"

"Nah, you'll be fine."

"Hopefully you will be too."

Yuri smirked. "See you around, maybe."

"Maybe."

Yuri shoved what he wasn't wearing into the plastic bags. Then he slipped out of the truck, barefoot, and shut the door behind him. He ran and didn't look back

VALENTINE'S DAY TIGERS

as the black and white spruces settled in around him. He continued running until he knew he was out of Ash's sight. Then he shifted.

It started as a tiny tremor at the base of his spine and was followed by the loud cracks of bones mystically reshaping. Orange fur striped with black sprouted over skin that stretched to cover a large frame of muscles, and he dropped to all fours. His powerful paws hit the earth, and the cold became nothing but a distant memory. His tail flicked behind him with another burst of energy. Life rippled through his body, his skin hummed, and he roared into the night because he was alive.

He was alive.

CHAPTER 6

IT WAS WELL PAST midnight, and Yuri hadn't called to tell Lance to pick him up yet. He'd have to eventually since Lance took the SUV, so Lance kept waiting and watching the time pass by at an agonizing pace.

Most people were in bed and sleeping by now.

Lance was starting to worry, but he didn't want to call first. Yuri had a cell phone because Lance insisted he take the one Lance bought him for situations similar to this one. Yuri always went along with it to placate his brother even though he didn't give a damn about cell phones; he could take them or leave them.

If not for the new and modernized Eurio, Lance

VALENTINE'S DAY TIGERS

would have been suffering alone in Fairbanks because his brother wouldn't have been able to get a call out to Lance's cell phone here. Now he had service. That was looking at the bright side, but it didn't help Lance's mood.

Maybe he shouldn't have gone back to Eurio anyway. It took an hour to drive to Fairbanks.

Whatever.

Yuri deserved it.

Lance was pissed off.

He let out a groan and sunk deeper into Austin and Mateo's couch. It wasn't very comfortable. The cushions didn't make the hard, wooden frame much softer, but he ignored the wood jamming into his back and kept going until he sank all the way to the rug on the floor. Then he just kind of melted there like a scoop of ice cream that had been dropped on the hot pavement in San Francisco.

It was a good thing he didn't live somewhere sunny. His skin wouldn't have liked that, but it didn't make much of a difference in the end. He was almost always wearing a hat of some kind outside, whether it was to keep the sun off his skin or to keep himself warm. Or both.

He groaned again.

"I don't get what you're doing here exactly," Austin said, pushing his glasses up the bridge of his nose. His pale face flushed. "Mateo and I were supposed to be in bed hours ago. And why are you groveling on the floor now?"

"Just because," Lance said.

"I'd understand if your house still looked like a bomb went off, but you've cleaned it out. It actually looks like a house."

Lance didn't say anything to that. There was no point in keeping any of that medical shit now that Yuri was better. He also didn't know why Austin was talking to him. Last he checked, Austin didn't like him or Yuri.

Mateo knelt in front of Lance and pushed Lance's shoulders so their eyes met. "You're making my mate anxious," Mateo said and cocked his head. "Are you on something?"

Lance snorted. "I wish."

Mateo went quiet. He searched Lance's eyes as if he were waiting for him to expand on that thought. Lance didn't. He said this instead: "You've changed. Since you came back from Utah with Austin, it's like you've become a different wolf. You never go out with me and Yuri anymore."

"You're not out with Yuri either. You didn't want

to 'get laid'?"

Lance closed his eyes to keep himself from screaming. Yuri hadn't done much with sex since they were teens because his seizures acted up and then the PWD hit.

"I just wonder. What's so great about sex?" Lance said. He meant to keep the thought to himself. He always had, but he let it slip.

His heart pounded in his chest when he realized what he had done. And he didn't say any more. That one question brought an eerie silence. Neither Austin nor Mateo said anything, and the seconds dragged on. Lance was reluctant to open his eyes until he got this under control. He had to keep a cool exterior. His secret had to be kept a secret. So, he forced his eyes open and said, "Calm down, guys. I was just kidding."

Mateo scowled. And he answered the question anyway. Sort of. "Because it feels good?" he said.

He stared at Lance for another moment, like he was still waiting for Lance to say something. Lance hated how he did that. Mateo took things differently than anyone else did. He saw things others didn't. That was probably why he had gotten along with Yuri and Lance when he first came to Eurio. They were like outsiders together, but Mateo was acting like Eurio was his home. He always had in a way that Yuri and Lance hadn't, but it was different now. He had no desire to cause trouble anymore. He wasn't angry and had no reason to get that adrenaline rush. His wolf was forever dicey, but Austin had him now. Mateo would go for a run if he needed to, but he did it alone, without getting anyone else ripped up in the process, and he was always eager to get back to his mate.

"You don't think so?" Mateo asked.

Lance rolled his eyes. "I mean, why is sex with your *mate* so great that you turned into another shifter?"

Austin shoved his glasses up the bridge of his nose again even though they hadn't fallen. He was dressed in plaid flannel pajamas and looked like a proper nerd. He frowned and folded his arms when Lance spent more than a second looking at him as if he were embarrassed Lance was seeing him like *this*.

"For the record, I don't have a problem with Austin. It was just confusing at first." Lance meant to say that to Austin himself, but he couldn't look the human in the eye. "You know, Mateo? It used to be you, me, and Yuri. You were ready to go anywhere with us, and we were ready to add Austin to the mix, but that went to hell in three seconds."

VALENTINE'S DAY TIGERS

"I don't dislike you," Austin defended. "But yeah, I don't really get all the stuff you like to do. Gale doesn't even know the extent of it, does he? You guys put yourselves in a lot of danger sometimes, you know? Mateo is bad enough, but Yuri especially… He takes things as far as they'll go, and I… I worry. I don't know what I'd do if Mateo got hurt." Lance knew that Austin worried about more than Mateo getting "hurt." He did that. Everything was the worst-case scenario with him.

"Yeah," Mateo scratched the back of his head, "I don't enjoy worrying my mate, and I don't feel like I need to do that stuff so much anymore."

"So, having a mate turns a shifter soft," Lance concluded.

"No. I do feel different, though. I used to be empty, but I don't feel empty anymore. Before, adrenaline was the only thing I could feel. Now Austin keeps me going, and it's not just about sex being good. It's everything about Austin."

Austin's face went cherry red, and he fixed his glasses with a nervous fury; he simultaneously knocked them over as he tried to push them up the bridge of his nose. Over and over. Lance had to look away from him. It was just too damn pitiful.

But he didn't get it either.

He didn't get Yuri's dangerous streaks that went beyond… well, beyond. But he would go along with almost anything because Yuri was his brother. At the very least, he had to be there for Yuri to keep him safe. Yuri was his world ever since their dad died. Even before that, Yuri had always been his world.

Lance bit the inside of his cheek.

Yuri was a loose cannon in a lot of ways, but he wouldn't do any of that crazy stuff with Ash, would he? He hadn't in the past. He would tell ladies what they wanted to hear, use his good looks and his charm to get sex. That was what he had planned for Ash, right? He was just joking around when he said—

Banging on the door jerked Lance out of his thoughts. Austin's face paled back to its normal white, and he grabbed the collar of his shirt in surprise. Mateo jumped up and answered the door. Yuri came rushing in without so much as a hello. He was half-dressed; he didn't even have a shirt on, let alone a coat.

"Did you run all the way back?!" Lance demanded. "You could've called me. I would've picked you up."

"I figured with the way you left all pissed off that you didn't want me around. And what are you doing *here*? I went home first, but you weren't there. Did you even get laid?"

VALENTINE'S DAY TIGERS

Lance wrinkled his nose. Lance didn't smell like sex. Granted, he could have come home and showered away the scent, but Yuri hadn't. He smelled like sex big time. And he smelled like Ash.

Lance didn't care. He really didn't. Or, he wouldn't have if he hadn't felt so threatened.

He shoved past Yuri and grabbed his coat. Then he was out the door, trudging through snow at a furious pace as he made his way home. Yuri could return the SUV to the Lodge. Fuck this. Ash wasn't even Yuri's type, and he had gone right for them with a laser focus. Lance couldn't take seeing Yuri make a move on Ash like that. He couldn't take the smell of sex. Because Yuri would win. Lance would be nothing but a memory to Ash if even that.

Yuri always won, no matter the obstacle, because he was real, and Lance was but a shadow.

It was cold and dark. Snow was underneath his paws. Yuri had no recollection of how he got here. He knew he had to have given his form over to his tiger, but he didn't remember doing so. And something felt off. The black and white spruces seemed bigger than he remembered, towering up into the sky

and nearly concealing it entirely.

He didn't know why he was running, but when he tried to stop, nothing happened. It was like his body had a mind of its own. He tried to turn his head to look behind him, but he couldn't get his head to move much. If he tried very hard, there would be some give, but then his head whipped back to the front.

He had no control.

His paws didn't look right either. They were a silvery white and narrower than he remembered, like a wolf's paws.

His head bent down, and his nose almost connected with the snow below as he sniffed and sniffed again. It was nothing but pure snow. Then he was running again.

Yuri let it, his body, take him. He didn't have much of a choice. It continued. He walked through snow, ran, stopped, and sniffed. He had to endure this same routine, over and over. His nose connected with the snow yet again, and he expected nothing. But then he smelled something strange. It burned his nose, crackled all the way up to his brain. It was familiar, too familiar, because he knew it and its destructive power too well: Black Magic.

When his body tried to move on its own again, Yuri roared in his head. He refused and imagined digging his feet in past the snow and into dirt, anchoring his body. And then his sight jumped out of his body. It made him dizzy. He

VALENTINE'S DAY TIGERS

couldn't focus at first, but then he could. His vision cleared, and he was like a specter floating in the sky as he looked down at where he once stood.

It wasn't his body at all.

The one in the snow, with the deep blue eyes Yuri had been looking through, was a humongous wolf. His eyes pierced through to Yuri's core, and Yuri's heart stuttered because they were just a little bit too *familiar.*

Yuri's mind seized up.

He gasped and shot up straight in bed. The vision was gone. There was nothing but familiar darkness creeping along the wooden corners and walls of his and Lance's rather empty room. Nothing looked out of place.

But there was an absence of warmth.

Yuri's hand reached out behind him for his brother, who should've been there at his side, but he wasn't. He sat up and grasped the blankets as if that would reveal his brother's location, as if Lance were hiding underneath them when Yuri knew that wasn't the case, but his brain and body insisted he search. He took in a shuddering breath and whispered, "Calm down."

That seemed to shock his mind and body into playing nice again. Yuri sighed, tightened his grip on the blanket for only a moment, and then let go. He closed his eyes and focused on a sound that caught his attention. It was a low rumble and a high hiss: running water.

It was morning, and Lance was just taking a shower.

Yuri plopped back down on the bed and rolled over, not bothering to cover himself or to fix the twisted blanket. He was going back to bed. Everything was fine.

Everything was fine.

CHAPTER 7

WARM WATER CASCADED OVER Lance, and he took a moment to enjoy it. He could've just stayed like that for the entirety of his shower—until he used up all the hot water—since he had already finished washing. But no, that wasn't what he was doing in here.

He took a breath and tried to pump himself up.

He hadn't done this in a while.

He stared down in between his legs and knew he could easily get it up by relaxing and handling himself, but wasn't it supposed to be even easier than that? Couldn't other guys get it up just by looking at someone they found attractive? Lance knew that was how

Yuri worked. If he saw some "hot chick," all the blood would rush to his dick. Lance was used to the smell of arousal. As shifters, this kind of knowledge was a free-for-all buried deep into their senses. It wasn't anything weird, and Lance never thought a thing about it before. He was aware of it—but he had never experienced it himself. Not like that.

Lance thought about Ash, conjuring up an image of them in his mind, and closed his eyes to focus only on them. He could see every detail clearly because he took them in whenever he was with them. That crazy beautiful rainbow hair, exactly how high their smile reached, the sparkle in their green eyes, all that smooth skin. He could picture Ash's typical outfit. It was always ripped up jeans and a tank top indoors. He tried to find a detail to focus on, one that would make this work.

Then he thought of it. Ash never wore a bra. He could visualize the outline of their breasts. Good. He could also recall the exact width of their hips, the curves in their legs, down to those boots lined in a furry synthetic material that Ash was so fond of. Okay, he shouldn't be thinking about the boots.

He went back to boobs and hips. They didn't really make him feel any different. Every part of Ash evoked warm memories. That warmth settled inside of his chest, but there wasn't any sort of epiphany in his dick. It was just Ash, and Ash gave him that fluttery feeling in his stomach.

Ash gave him butterflies, like that song they sang at Tipsy. Was that song about him? It couldn't be…

Focus, idiot, Lance berated himself and shook his head.

Maybe the key was to imagine Ash naked, then.

Lance went through that checklist again, visualizing Ash from head to toe, naked this time. But he immediately got stuck. He'd never seen Ash naked before. He had an idea of what they'd look like. He knew they had the body of a female, but imagining a basic female body wasn't working. He knew how female bodies worked. He had seen females naked plenty of times due to shifting, but it was never anything other than them being naked. It was never anything sexual.

So, his thoughts drifted. They went to Drew.

Lance remembered Drew very well. It was hard not to. When he and Yuri were sixteen, before the seizure that drastically changed Yuri's life for so many years, Yuri had been as flighty as he was now. He looked for new people to meet, crashed parties, and picked up chicks. All of that was happening again. And, like back then, Lance went along with him

At sixteen, Fairbanks was the place to be. It was the biggest city the twins could get to in the least amount of time. Once they got there, they'd split up. Yuri would find a girl to run off with, and Lance would usually busy himself with something quieter. They'd have phones or they'd arrange to meet at a certain time and place, and that was that. Lance wasn't a socialite like Yuri, but he did end up in scrappy, small clubs (some of them allowed sixteen-year-olds and others didn't) until Yuri found someone who caught his interest and went off on his own. It was during one of those times that Lance met Drew.

They were both wallflowers at a club where their age was acceptable. It had shoddy strobing lights that were starting to give Lance a headache. Yuri had just left, so Lance didn't plan on sticking around. Then Drew happened. Lance saw him out of the corner of his eye, a smiley boy who was a little bit taller than he was. Lance was prepared to ignore him. People tended to stare at Lance. They told him he looked weird because of his albinism. He even turned his back when Drew held up his hand and said a short, "H-hey!"

The guy visibly shrunk when Lance gave his usual cold shoulder. But he seemed harmless enough, and Yuri was always out meeting new people, so maybe

VALENTINE'S DAY TIGERS

Lance should put in an effort. Lance turned back to face Drew and said, "Hey."

The guy's face lit up like there was a lightbulb hidden somewhere down his throat. "Y-you alone?" he asked.

"Yeah."

"W-want to dance?"

Lance liked how he stuttered. He knew it was because the guy was nervous. The tiger side of him was sensitive to all kinds of emotions. It wasn't a bad nervous, though. He wasn't going to stand there and make fun of Lance because of how he looked.

"Oh! God, sorry. I'm Drew by the way." His sun-kissed cheeks went such a bright red they put the cheap strobe-lights to shame. He held out his hand to Lance; it trembled, but he didn't back down.

"Lance." Instead of making the guy suffer, Lance took his hand and shook it.

Drew was warm and bubbly when he took Lance out on the rather empty dance floor. Lance didn't think too much of him at first, but he had fun. Lance never had any desire to know anyone outside of Yuri, but Drew was interesting. He was a chatterbox, and his smile was infectious. He was a little bit like Yuri in that way.

But he was also nothing like Yuri.

When Lance and Drew had danced their fill, the two of them were starving. Drew insisted on buying Lance dinner, and Lance let him. They both got a burger and fries, but Lance's fries looked a ton better. Drew's were the soggy sad bunch that were old and should have been thrown out while Lance's were crisp and freshly fried.

"Want one?" Lance asked.

He was teasing. He thought nothing of it as he held a fry out to Drew, and Drew took it right out of Lance's hand with his teeth. It sent a rush through Lance; a fluttering sensation filled his stomach as this guy gave him the stupidest grin. But he was cute. And Lance liked hearing his stories.

"Can I have your number?" Drew asked.

Lance mulled it over. He didn't mind, but he didn't normally have service. Gale didn't even know he and Yuri had cell phones. They were cheap flip phones, but still. No one in Eurio had one except for Iris, but she was hardly ever in Eurio since she was off on Trinity business.

Lance closed his eyes, drifting out of his memories for a moment as the water from the showerhead pounded his eyelids. He wouldn't admit it, but Iris's

VALENTINE'S DAY TIGERS

death had been hard for him. He knew it had been many times worse for Gale, but Iris was the reason Lance and Yuri were safe in Eurio. He'd always be grateful to her, even if he had never shown it properly.

So, Lance had mulled Drew's question over. He ended up saying yes. From then on, when Yuri wanted to go out, Lance found a way to see Drew again. They planned places to meet up whenever it was time for Lance to go home, and they talked on their phones when they could. Lance never told Drew much concerning his truths, but he started to know Drew, and Drew started to know him. Regardless of outside details, shifters and humans, their souls were made bare.

Yuri never asked questions and never cared, so he never officially met Drew. He likely didn't even know he existed, seeing as Lance and Yuri only met up at the end of their escapades to drive back to Eurio. Lance was more private than Yuri. It took him time to process things just like it took him a long time to warm up to people. Yuri never stayed with any one person for long, never long enough to know them. Each time they went to Fairbanks, he was out to find someone new. He likely assumed Lance was doing the same thing.

That went on for weeks. During that time, just thinking about Drew gave Lance butterflies.

One time, when Lance and Drew snuck into a back room of the same scrappy club they had first met, Drew kissed Lance for the first time. Lance was surprised, but he didn't move back. They were alone, just him and Drew, and everything felt safe enough.

Drew said, "I was worried you wouldn't let me kiss you. I was starting to think these feelings are all one-sided."

"What do you mean?" Lance asked.

"I like you."

"I like you, too."

Drew kissed him again after that. Lance had never kissed anyone before. It was a sloppy mess, awkward with noses bumping, but he got the hang of it with Drew's help.

"I keep forgetting you're only sixteen," said Drew.

"Sorry," was all Lance could think to say back. It wasn't like Drew was that much older than him. He was seventeen.

Drew laughed. "Why are you apologizing?" He placed his hands on Lance's hips and kissed him again. This kiss was different. It wasn't a question. It was a demand. And Lance wasn't sure he liked it. The first kisses were lips brushing softly together. It made the butterflies in his stomach fly up and into his rib cage.

VALENTINE'S DAY TIGERS

His heart beat faster. But this kiss was hard, teeth biting, and Drew's tongue fighting its way inside of Lance's mouth. Drew pulled back before Lance could figure out how he wanted to retaliate.

"I love you," Drew said. "I don't just like you."

Then it hit him. Lance realized he must have loved Drew, too. He had never let himself love anyone before, anyone outside of Yuri, but he did love Drew. He kept coming back to him. He anticipated seeing him, and the butterflies were there with every thought of him. It was hard for him to understand since he had become so detached. He and Yuri had to live that way to survive growing up on the streets. They never trusted anyone outside of themselves. Even all their time spent in Eurio, it was just the two of them. They stayed safe inside of their little duo, and then Lance let Drew in.

"I love you, too," Lance said. And he knew it was true because of the butterflies, because he never let anybody else in like this, because he felt a warmth with Drew that was very different from what he felt toward his brother. This had to be romantic love, the thing he'd seen floating around in Eurio, the thing he'd seen between Gale and Iris. He understood it now.

"I locked the door, so unless somebody with the

key tries to get in here, we have this room all to ourselves," Drew said.

"Okay?" Lance shrugged.

Drew took off his shirt. He went for his pants next, but then he looked up at Lance with red cheeks. "Don't make me strip all by myself. It's embarrassing."

Lance thought to ask what they were doing, but he didn't want to seem stupid or any more inexperienced than he obviously was. So, he stripped off his shirt too, and a wave of arousal hit his nose the same moment Drew stared at him with wide eyes.

"Hell, you are ripped," Drew said.

Lance had caught whiffs of arousal before, especially between mates, but he never had a word for it until recently. It wasn't until Yuri had started getting so interested in sex that his brother "educated" him on things. Lance knew Yuri's sexual interest had partly to do with their age and partly to do with the fact that they felt safe enough to be regular teens to some extent, since settling as well as they had into Eurio.

Yuri liked sex jokes, and Lance had to work to keep up. They often went over his head, but he was good at pretending, and he figured things out at some point.

Drew stepped forward and touched Lance's chest.

VALENTINE'S DAY TIGERS

"You're so warm."

Lance stayed quiet. He observed Drew's palm eclipsing the space above his heart. It made his heart sputter. He caught Drew's brown-eyed gaze and was content to hold it, to let unspoken feelings pass between them.

But he hadn't known then that they weren't operating on the same wavelength.

CHAPTER 8

DREW WENT FOR LANCE'S pants, and Lance let him. He assisted him until they were both naked in front of each other. Drew took the opportunity to look at Lance from head to toe. Lance followed his lead once again and returned the look. He hadn't seen Drew naked before. Maybe he was supposed to think something of it because that odd sugary scent permeated the air. It was thick, even tangy on his tongue.

"You are so hot," Drew said. He stepped forward again and touched Lance's hips. It was a sensitive area that Lance never let anybody but Drew touch, especially not like this, and it made his skin jump.

"And you're so pale," Drew commented. "It's like

VALENTINE'S DAY TIGERS

you're made of snow and ice." Lance was about to tell him to shut the hell up because he had had more than his fair share of nasty comments when it came to his albinism. But then Drew said, "You're beautiful."

Drew trailed his fingers down Lance's skin, to his thigh, and Lance felt a buzz. He didn't mind Drew touching him softly like this, but he didn't really know what they were doing, or why he seemed so fixated on Lance's dick.

"Soft," Drew's cheeks were on fire.

"So?" Lance asked.

Drew took himself in hand. He was hard, and his face went even redder. "Don't like what you see?"

"What are you talking about? I love what I see." Lance reached up and held the back of Drew's head. Lance was not short for his age, but that year Drew had on him meant Drew was just a little bit taller, for now. Drew took the invitation to kiss Lance again, the aggressive kind. He stepped forward, and Lance stumbled back until his back was pressed into a wall. Drew kissed him deeper. This time he rocked his hips against Lance's. Lance wasn't sure what he thought about that. It was new, and he was starting to get hard with the friction.

Drew breathed heavily as he moved back and took

Lance in hand. Lance shuddered and grabbed Drew's shoulders to steady himself. Something was building, and Lance needed… something.

"There we go," Drew said.

Lance's breaths came quicker, shallower.

"Ready to feel good?" Drew asked.

"I guess," Lance said, but in all honesty, he wasn't feeling that good at all. There was a tension concentrated in his dick that got worse as it built. He'd masturbated every now and then, but it was just because it was something he had discovered in the shower when he was bored one day.

Drew must not have heard the hesitation in his voice, and Lance was too willing to let Drew lead. There were some cushions in the room that Drew pressed Lance down on. Lance was stronger than Drew. He knew this, but he was paralyzed for some reason. He couldn't act, couldn't put words to this sense of dread, because Drew seemed so happy. Lance wanted him happy. This was what two people who were in love did, right?

"Do you trust me?" Drew asked.

"Yeah," Lance said. That was also true. Lance hadn't trusted anybody but Yuri before, but he had let Drew in. He trusted him. Maybe he shouldn't have.

VALENTINE'S DAY TIGERS

"This might hurt a little at first, but it will start feeling really good in a minute, okay?"

"Okay," Lance said, but his heart was beating a million miles an hour, and it had nothing to do with butterflies. He was starting to panic. This was a submissive position he took with no one. And Drew was still touching him, trailing fingers down sensitive skin. It burned in an uncomfortable way.

Drew spread Lance's legs so he could crawl on top of him. He moved Lance back so that he could get whatever meticulous positioning he wanted, and then he pressed his dick into Lance's ass. At first, it was very shallow, but Lance immediately didn't like it. Then Drew rolled his hips. Lance seized up and then grabbed at Drew's hips to make him stop.

"What are you doing?" Lance gasped.

"It'll get better. Promise," Drew said.

Lance held fast to Drew's hips, but he didn't stop Drew from rolling his hips forward again. This time Drew buried himself deeper. There was no lubrication, no nothing. It was painful.

"Stop," Lance said. "I don't like it." All the butterflies in his stomach died. They fell to the base of his stomach like rocks.

"Sorry," Drew said, wide-eyed. "Oh, I know what's

wrong." He stared down at Lance thoughtfully as he moved back a little, but not far enough to let Lance up. "Let's do something else instead."

Lance was about to say he didn't want to, but Drew's hands went around Lance's length, building friction, building that tension into an unbelievably uncomfortable pressure. Lance gritted his teeth. He held on to Drew like he was the only thing keeping him from drowning and tried not to dig into Drew's skin with claws that demanded to show face. And he just... held on. He wanted it to be over already. He wanted the pressure to release.

"A guy did this for me once," Drew said.

And still, Lance couldn't speak. His head was swimming as Drew's lips went around him and he slowly took Lance farther and farther until it would have required him swallowing to go any more. His tongue was hot and wet, burning sensitive nerve endings. Lance writhed.

Sweat poured down Lance's skin as he tried to remember how to breathe, how to talk. He could get away. He could push Drew away and get the hell out of there, but none of it made sense. This was the same Drew Lance said he loved and meant it. He wasn't being malicious. Lance could sense it. He was excited,

VALENTINE'S DAY TIGERS

eager to please, and *none* of it made sense.

Finally, to Lance's great relief, he climaxed. Drew backed up, startled as he choked on the hot liquid dripping from his mouth. He wiped his mouth with the back of his hand, and Lance shuddered his relief.

"You should have warned me you were close," Drew said.

Lance was too busy shaking his head to reply to that. Drew plopped down onto the cushion beside Lance, and then Lance started wondering how sanitary these things were, and how many other people had gone back here to do this same thing.

"Feel good?" Drew asked.

Lance didn't know how to answer that.

"Do you think you could help me get off?"

Lance sat up. He glanced at Drew, at his face, the face he adored and dreamed about when he went to bed at night. Drew had comforting brown eyes, eyes Lance trusted, and stubble he was letting grow because he wanted to try out a beard. Then Lance looked down at Drew's hard-on.

"Sure," Lance said. And he would, because he saw the stars in Drew's eyes, like this meant something to him, something beyond compare.

Lance took Drew's length and gently rubbed,

watching Drew's reactions; his face went slack and scrunched up at the same time, and he squeezed his eyes shut.

"Oh, man, I'm so close," Drew said. "You want to try? I'll walk you through it. Please."

Lance hesitated. "This isn't good enough?"

"Seriously?" Drew frowned.

"Okay, I'll try it."

They switched positions. Lance pushed away the repulsion he felt as he took Drew into his mouth. It was something about the bitter taste.

"Take me as far as you can go," Drew said between labored breaths. "Try using your tongue like I did."

Lance did as he said. He didn't know if he was doing it right since Drew started twitching almost like he was in pain on the cushion, but he must've been since Drew kept mumbling for him to continue. His hands were in Lance's hair, pulling, ripping.

"Going to come," Drew gasped.

Lance took that as his cue to back off. He waited safely to the side as Drew finished. Drew stayed panting on the cushions and Lance stood. He watched the rise and fall of Drew's chest and felt estranged, like an apparition floating around in the air. Lance wanted to go back out to the club. He wanted to dance. He wanted

VALENTINE'S DAY TIGERS

to share drinks like they usually did. He wanted to play the game where they tried to feed each other. Those thoughts brought the butterflies back to life.

"What are you doing?" Drew asked as he pushed himself up. "Why are you just standing there staring?"

"I don't know," Lance confessed.

"You didn't like that at all, did you?" And suddenly Drew's scent went sour. The mood changed like the dull throbbing of the bass beats outside of the room.

"You did," Lance pointed out.

"That wasn't what I asked."

Lance shrugged. "Let's get dressed and head back out. I'm hungry."

"Look," Drew said as his eyes went down to the ground. He wrapped his arms around himself like he was suddenly embarrassed to be naked in front of Lance. "It's fine if you don't feel the same way. I just wish you had told me sooner. Before... I can't be friends with you anymore, Lance. I like you too much. I thought you felt the same way I did."

"I do. I love you," Lance reminded.

"Don't lie. You don't love me." Drew clenched his hands into fists and bit his bottom lip so hard Lance thought it might bleed.

"Drew."

Lance reached out for him, but Drew shied away and shouted, "Don't touch me!"

Lance was taken aback. He moved away and sidled against a wall, giving Drew as much space as he needed. Lance knew how hard it was to let people in, and he knew the importance of giving them space when they asked for it. He knew the importance of needing to be alone to figure things out because he did that all the time. He watched Drew dress in a hurry, without a word, and then he watched him as he left Lance alone in the room.

Lance never saw Drew again after that.

CHAPTER 9

LANCE SLAMMED HIS HANDS against the shower wall. He leaned into the slippery tile, using his arms as a cushion as he rested his forehead there. He felt like he was suffocating in all the hot steam. He let out a breath.

"Focus," he told himself.

He tried to think of Ash again. He tried to use nothing but his mind to get that tension going, to coax a hard-on, but it didn't work when he thought about Ash. It only worked if he thought about sex itself, not even sex, just the thought of being aroused. But he wasn't interested in that now, and he was too upset to bother trying. It didn't matter anyway. He knew he could jerk off. There was nothing wrong with his body. It was something else.

Lance got out of the shower and dried himself off, then he threw the towel over the shower rack as he stepped out of the bathroom and into the hall where he met Yuri. He tried to move past his brother to get to their room, but Yuri blocked the way with his arms.

"Do you mind?" Lance asked. "I'd like to get my clothes on before I freeze to death."

"You're fine. It's not that cold in here," Yuri said. "We should go to Fairbanks again, and you should talk to the singer at Tipsy. Ash is hot as fuck, a real wildfire. They said they'd be moving on soon, but I bet we could catch them if we went again tonight."

Lance interrupted, "It's unusual for you to be this interested in someone. I don't think you've ever talked about seeing someone a second time in your life. They've all been nothing but conquests or something, but you actually want to *see* this one again?" A sour taste filled Lance's mouth. He didn't enjoy talking about Ash like this. He also didn't enjoy talking about Ash like he didn't know them.

Yuri shrugged. "Ash is sexy. Really sexy. That body, Lance."

VALENTINE'S DAY TIGERS

A hot body. Yuri was very straight. Ash had a feminine body. They were non-binary, but that didn't change the physical truth. And Yuri had the hots for them big time. What did that mean? Was Yuri falling in love with them?

The taste in Lance's mouth got worse.

"You haven't talked to me since we came home. And you're pissy now," Yuri said. "What's got your dick in a twist?"

Don't ask, Lance told himself. *Don't ask Yuri what he did with Ash. You don't want to know. And why did Yuri wear a shirt to bed? He never does that.*

"If looks could kill, bro." Yuri folded his arms. "Why are you so pissed off?"

"I'm not," Lance said. But he was. He was very pissed off. He shoved past Yuri and dodged as Yuri made to grab him. He made it to the bedroom and locked the door so Yuri couldn't come in.

"Seriously, Lance. I know you. What's wrong?"

Lance ground his teeth together. Luckily for him, he had some extra winter clothes inside the bedroom that were kept separate from the coat rack in the living room. He couldn't face Yuri right now. He pulled open the window just as he heard Yuri getting the spare key, and he left.

He trudged through the snow with a purpose. His end destination would be the Lodge so he could grab an SUV. He was going to prove Drew wrong. Drew said that Lance hadn't loved him. That wasn't true. Lance had. A part of him always would. And now he loved Ash. He would *prove* it. He would ask Ash to be his Valentine. He had to make a move before Yuri stole them away because Lance truly believed Yuri could have anyone he wanted. He was like that. *Magnetic*.

He was glad, ecstatic really, that Yuri was better, but that meant change. That meant Lance couldn't stay in this life forever or he would end up alone. Yuri would find a mate, and he would leave Lance sooner rather than later. How would he not? There was literally nothing holding him back anymore. It would be like Mateo, but much worse.

Lance gave everything to Yuri. Lance's identity was combined with Yuri's, even more so after Yuri got so sick. Lance had resigned himself to the fact that *that* would be the way it would always be, that Yuri would always need him and that Lance would always have a place to belong.

That didn't mean, during all this time, that Lance hadn't wanted more than that.

Drew broke Lance's heart. Lance had called and

waited for him for days after he said the words Lance would never forget. Lance tried to find him every time he and Yuri went back to Fairbanks. Yuri just kept on doing what he always did while Lance suffered alone and with the eventual realization that he would never see Drew again. The pain cut deep because Lance needed Drew. Maybe he always needed someone outside of Yuri, someone like… a mate. Lance wanted out of Yuri's shadow, and he wanted Ash.

But he was afraid.

It wasn't easy for him to connect with others. He didn't just have a revelation and decide he loved Ash after a couple days. It took months. Even with Drew. He wasn't like most people. Cedar and Gale hit it off immediately. They had this "chemistry," or so people said, and Lance didn't know what that meant other than arousal. He could relate to the butterflies metaphor, but he didn't get the *chemistry*.

But he was going to learn. He would make it work. He had to overcome this obstacle because it wasn't an obstacle for anyone else. He'd either adapt, or he'd end up alone.

Ash walked into the library. They didn't know why. Maybe it was to reminisce. It was partly that, and it was partly hope that Lance would be there because this was the last time. After this, Ash needed to move on with their life. If Lance wasn't who they had been searching for on this long road trip, then Fairbanks had nothing left to offer them. Alaska had nothing left to offer them.

They walked past familiar bookcases. It was quiet as usual with people studying at tables and wearing headphones. Ash was looking for a specific table, the one Lance always sat at. It was hidden in a corner and hardly ever seemed to be occupied unless Lance was there.

Ash found him here by chance once when they were getting out of the cold for a minute. It was Ash's first time in the library, so they really scoured the place. They tended to do that. It made for the best songs, observation that is. Lance had been at this corner table piled high with a ton of different books about the brain, seizures, and how brains process speech. When asked about it, he gave Ash some vague answer about the brain being fascinating.

Ash had pulled out a chair and sat down next to him. They rested their elbows on the wood surface and folded their arms in front of them. They got the truth

VALENTINE'S DAY TIGERS

out of Lance eventually—or as much of the truth as he was inclined to give apparently. No, that wasn't fair to say. It was the truth. Ash saw the difference in him.

The reason Lance spent so much time in the library was because he was researching a rare disorder called pure word deafness. His twin brother had it. Lance said he was pretty sick sometimes with seizures. One of those seizures was responsible for his PWD. Sometimes, they would make him bedridden, but, from what Lance said, Yuri was a fighter. He kept holding on, stubbornly refusing to let go.

Ash sat down and ran their hand across the table's glossy finish as if that would allow them to feel some residual heat Lance had left behind. But it was cold. No one had been here.

Ash wondered if Lance's brother had passed on or if his condition had gotten much worse. Those would've been valid reasons for him to disappear. And it wasn't as if he and Ash were in some sort of committed relationship. It wasn't as if Ash really understood what that was anyway. They had never concerned themself with such thoughts before. People came and went. Ash was used to that. Lance was the closest relationship they had ever had to anyone, and Ash wanted to keep what Lance made them realize they wanted more than an endless road trip.

Spending last night with mysterious Yuri cleared Ash's head. That was why they were at the library, giving Lance one more chance before they left. Yeah, they had some burns that twinged whenever their clothes rubbed them wrong, but it was a good hurt. It reminded them of the most important thing: they were *alive*, and so they were going to live with everything they had.

Ash smiled and tapped the table. "Right, Yuri?"

Well, that was enough reminiscing. Ash gave it one more shot, but Lance wasn't here. Ash wasn't going to pay for another night at the hotel. It was getting pricey. They had gotten a good deal, though, since Frank apparently knew the hotel owner. But enough was enough. It was time to move on.

Ash was about to get up, but shivers broke out across their skin when they heard *his* voice. "Ash."

Ash stood anyway, nails digging into the wooden table. They knew that voice very well, but they didn't want to turn around and be disappointed in case their mind was playing tricks on them. So, Ash took a deep breath and worked up the courage to take a peek. Sure enough, Lance was right there. His eyes were ice with lava underneath just waiting to burn through to the

VALENTINE'S DAY TIGERS

surface. The corners of his lips upturned slightly. Ash wouldn't have seen it if they hadn't learned to see Lance's smiles, even the smallest of the small. At first, even these smiles were hard to get out of him. But as they spent more time together, Lance had started giving them freely. Real smiles.

"Lance. It's been over a month since I last saw you."

"Were you looking for me?"

Ash folded their arms and decided not to answer that question. They deserved an explanation.

Lance's gaze darted to the ground before bouncing back up to meet Ash's eyes. "I'm sorry. My brother got really sick, and I couldn't leave him. But I'm back. I was always going to come back." The way he said that made Ash wonder if he said that last part for himself or for them. There was always something in Lance that wasn't ready to commit to this strange relationship he and Ash had been developing.

"Why didn't you wait for me?" he asked.

Ash's throat grew tight, and their hands clenched into fists of their sides. "I did wait."

They had. And they were here now, weren't they? What did Lance really mean anyway? He couldn't have known about Yuri last night. He wasn't there, and why

90

should he care? They hadn't talked about or had sex.

But Ash felt it: chemistry. Ash and Lance had done things only "lovers" did. Dates, stolen touches, longing looks. It had to be true. Ash and Lance felt the same way about each other, but they were both afraid to take it any further because of this emotional connection they had developed. Sex with Yuri was just sex. Sex with Lance would be something much more, something Ash had never before experienced.

"I did wait," Ash said again.

Lance shook his head, and now he wouldn't look Ash in the eye. "Forget I said that. I want to take you out, Ash. Karaoke. You said you wanted to do karaoke last time, but then stuff happened, and we didn't get to it."

The fact that Lance remembered that after weeks apart reminded Ash why they had fallen so hard for him, not to mention the fact that they could hardly take their eyes off him.

Lance had albinism. It was something he got stares for, and there were rude whispers every now and then, but Ash couldn't understand why. Lance was beautiful. Gorgeous. He had mentioned before that the sun was not his friend, but he otherwise didn't like talking about his skin, hair, or eyes. Ash had to bleach their hair

VALENTINE'S DAY TIGERS

hardcore to get white, but Lance's hair was practically white already. God, his physique. Ash didn't know how he could manage to look so lean and so muscular at the same time. Ash had only been with one person as ripped as Lance appeared to be: mysterious Yuri.

Ash frowned. They had seen a few of the tattoos Lance had covering his skin on rare occasions when it was hot enough for Lance to strip down to a tank top, including a white tiger tattooed on his left shoulder. It had to be a coincidence.

Lance was a mystery himself in so many ways.

There had been plenty of times on their dates when Ash had hoped stolen touches and glances would turn into something more because Ash would have been ready. They were ready now. If Lance wanted to take them away, after karaoke, everything would be perfect. More than perfect. It would be a dream.

Could Ash keep Lance? Was that a possibility?

Lance scratched the back of his head, still unwilling to meet Ash's eyes. "I don't sing, but, you know, I'll do it for you."

"You say that, and then you're going to end up being this fabulous singer and I'm going to be jealous." Ash took a step toward Lance. It was partly to close the distance between them and partly to make it so they didn't have to talk so loud; the two of them were drawing eyes.

Ash pressed forward until they were mere inches from touching Lance. He didn't move. He was rigid like ice. So, Ash took his hand and squeezed. Finally, Lance looked at them. A real smile lit up his face as he squeezed Ash's hand back. And yanked. He wrapped his other arm around Ash's back as he hugged them. He rested his cheek on the top of Ash's head.

"God, I missed you," he said.

Ash closed their eyes. They breathed in through their nose, catching Lance's subtle scent, something they were only privileged with when they were close like this. Ash had tried to find something to compare his scent to, but they couldn't come up with anything other than it was earthy. Maybe a type of flower?

"I missed you, too," Ash said. "How's your brother doing?"

"He's okay. He's really okay. In fact, he's going to be just fine now. His PWD is gone, and he hasn't had a seizure since."

Ash hugged him as tightly as they could. His body was so hard, there was hardly any give. "Really? That's great. I'm so happy for him and for you."

VALENTINE'S DAY TIGERS

And Ash was filled with the promise of the possibilities that brought with it. Maybe this meant Lance was ready for more.

CHAPTER 10

"YOU REALLY GAVE ME the slip," Yuri muttered. He was giving up the chase. Lance had doubled around and messed up his trail fantastically. It wasn't until Yuri made it to the Lodge and saw that one of the SUVs was missing that he realized what Lance had done. He wondered if Lance had asked for the keys and if Gale had given them freely, or if Lance had hot-wired the thing. Lately, Gale gave up the keys.

Whatever, Yuri thought. It didn't matter now. The fact was Lance had left Eurio, and he hadn't wanted Yuri to know.

"What am I supposed to do with myself?" Yuri wondered aloud.

VALENTINE'S DAY TIGERS

He stared at the refined logs making up the back-side of the Lodge. Then he peeked around the corner. There was something going on inside the building. He had kept out of sight, but he had seen some shifters coming and going from the front when he had made his way back here. He decided to check it out, but not by going through the front door.

Yuri found a cracked-open window in the back that led into the kitchen. He smelled chocolate. The room was empty at the moment, and the lights were turned off. Cedar was obsessing over Valentine's Day, and making chocolates was something she invited everybody to do at the meeting yesterday. Yuri remembered that now. Apparently, that was today.

Yuri opened the window wider and slipped inside. His boots hardly made a sound when they touched down on hard tiles. Stealth was a tiger shifter's best friend. The door to the kitchen didn't open, so no one heard Yuri enter. The chocolates were sitting out in the open. Cooling, he guessed. Some of them were inside of heart molds, others were on the counter, and others sat inside red-ribboned boxes.

He could hear voices if he craned his ears, but he was otherwise alone.

"Lucky me," Yuri said.

It seemed like Cedar went all out on the chocolate production. There were chocolates lined up to every shade. There were white chocolates too. Yuri would avoid those and anything that wasn't dark chocolate. He never got why people liked milk chocolate. It never tempted him. And white chocolate was just gross.

He grabbed a piece of dark chocolate that was shaped like a heart (surprise) and took a bite. It had a raspberry filling that complemented the cocoa. It made his taste buds sing. Contented, he hummed and went for a double-heart piece of dark chocolate. Soon he was taking one from each batch, even ones he wouldn't normally take. Cedar was a master with anything cooking, wasn't she? Food in Eurio had never tasted so good.

Yuri just popped another chocolate heart into his mouth when the kitchen door opened. He almost choked on it. So much for paying attention to his surroundings. But then he realized why. It was just Ike. He didn't have his radar up for little kids. They passed through his defenses because they were usually easily swayed. Yuri pounded his chest with his fist to get the chocolate out of his throat. Then he crushed it with his teeth and swallowed it properly this time.

"Yuri?" Ike said. The little polar bear cub stared at

VALENTINE'S DAY TIGERS

him with wide gray eyes.

"Hey, Ike."

"What are you doing?"

"Nothing much. Tasting some chocolates. You gonna join me?" Yuri popped another chocolate heart into his mouth and chewed. It had a creamy mint filling. He didn't know which one was his favorite. They were all so good.

"No, I came in to grab something for Cedar." Ike picked up a velvety red box and then cocked his head. "That isn't very nice. We worked hard on those chocolates."

"Hey, I haven't taken more than one from anybody's stash," Yuri said. "And there's a fuckton of these. They're not going to miss them, promise. Here," Yuri snatched up another chocolate heart he hadn't tried yet and held it out to Ike, "you can try this one."

The cub's mouth watered.

"It isn't going to kill anyone," Yuri urged.

Ike almost took it, but then he shook his head. "If you had come earlier, you would've gotten to try them while we were making them. Want to make your own?"

"Too late. I missed the party, right?"

"Cedar won't mind. She'll get you started on your own batch. And then you can make a card."

"Hell no. That is okay." Yuri popped the chocolate heart into his mouth. This one had an orange filling. Best yet? Maybe.

"That's one of the ones Austin made for Mateo," Ike said.

Yuri reflexively spit out the chocolate into his hand. "Oh, good. Another reason for Austin to hate me." He shrugged and put the chocolate back into his mouth. He ruined it now anyway with all his saliva. He wiped his hand on his pants.

As soon as he swallowed the treat, a strange pain shot up into his skull, like fireworks just burst inside his brain. He winced and grabbed his head. It was sudden, seemingly random, but the worst part was the familiarity. This was the kind of pain that visited him at the onset of a seizure. He hadn't had any problems since Josh worked his magic on him and cured him almost a month ago.

"Cured."

He thought he was over this shit.

Yuri was dizzy. He caught himself on the counter, but not before shoving a good portion of the chocolates off as he fell to his chest. Pans and boxes went too, causing a big clatter. His vision spun, and he saw double.

VALENTINE'S DAY TIGERS

Ike stepped back, and then shifters were streaming into the kitchen like ants. They were saying things, but Yuri didn't know what. He couldn't understand a word of it. It was a garbled mess like incoherent screaming.

He shook his head and shook it again, trying to listen to what they were saying.

Gale was the one he heard first. "Yuri, really?"

"What are you doing?" Cedar said.

Good. He could understand them again. That was all Yuri needed to know. Now he needed to take care of this pain, but he couldn't think about anything but the pain. This familiar scratching on his skull, sparks nestling in his brain...

He shifted, right then and there. It hurt when it wasn't supposed to. He felt every fracture in his bones like they were being crushed by sledgehammers. It was somehow worse when they rearranged themselves and his muscle tissue formed over them like his body was being coated in lava. His black-striped orange fur cut through him like millions of tiny needles. He didn't even realize it was over until the sound of shrieking ceramic pierced his ears; his claws dug grooves into the kitchen tiles.

Someone was about to lunge for him. He couldn't

100

make out who it was, and he turned. There wasn't enough room for his big body. He swept off whatever was left on the counter with his tail like a wild broom. He ran like a drunken cat and somehow made it out the window without getting stuck. He had a bit of a rough landing, though, when his legs collapsed underneath him, but he got back up.

Yuri did his best to run through the snow after that; however, committing to a straight line was basically impossible. His vision continued to produce double, so he bent forward and ran his head through the snow. He kept moving like that, somehow avoiding bashing his skull into the trunk of a black or white spruce even though he couldn't see a damn thing. The cold slowly penetrated his skull, and the pain numbed.

He just had to wait it out. He had to embrace the pain because he was still alive. He would make it through like he always did. He would conquer this.

CHAPTER 11

ASH CLAPPED AS LANCE finished his song. It took a while for him to warm up and finally sing, so Ash had been singing double time, and that was fine. They didn't mind singing for hours on end, but Ash wouldn't stand for Lance being a wallflower forever. It was just the two of them, and he said he'd sing. And he did. Oh, he did.

"That was amazing!" Ash said. They ran up to Lance in their tiny private karaoke room and wrapped their arms around his neck. "I thought you said you couldn't sing."

The room was hot and sweat beaded on Lance's skin like melting ice. "I said I don't sing," he corrected.

"Well, you have a great voice. Now you have to start singing with me. We can become a duo." Ash tapped his chest with a couple of fingers. Then, after taking in a sharp breath, they laid their hand over his heart. "Deep and sexy and a little husky too."

Lance smirked, but then the expression fell away. Ash stepped back, giving him space. Something seemed off about him tonight, but also not. There were moments where it was all familiar territory, but there was still some sort of impassable barrier between them. Ash would be the first to admit that it was partly their own fault.

Ash wanted to do the impossible tonight. They wanted to break through the barrier.

Hesitantly, Ash wrapped their arms around the back of Lance's neck again, inviting him closer. Lance didn't flinch away. He met Ash's gaze with ice-blue eyes and placed his hand on their waist. Ash wanted both of his hands, but one of them still held the microphone. It didn't matter in the end. They could look into each other's eyes for minutes, without saying a word, and it felt comfortable. More than comfortable. Ash had never had this kind of relationship with anyone. Whatever *this* was.

That was when Ash could pinpoint what felt

VALENTINE'S DAY TIGERS

wrong. Lance had a hard time keeping eye contact tonight.

"My turn," Ash said as they took the mic from Lance's hand. They untangled themselves, and Lance sat down on the bench as Ash stood at the front of the room near the screen. They skimmed through the titles to find a sweet love song. They bypassed Korean or Japanese and went straight for English so Lance would understand.

Ash succeeded in finding a song they had heard on the radio before. It fit the criteria well enough for now. Later, Ash would sing the song they wrote, but not yet. When the time came, it would be even quieter, even more private. It'd be just Ash with their ukulele serenading the man who gave them butterflies.

After the song started, Ash sang the first line with ease. They memorized music rather effortlessly and were pleased with their pick. This song was about seeing a cute guy across the street and getting up the courage to talk to him. That one little thing then spiraled into one of those fairytale romances.

Yeah, this was a good song. It described pretty well how Ash felt. Their heart beat faster with the realization. Their hands were even clammy. It was a first for Ash. This was the kind of stuff people experienced when it came to stage fright, but Ash didn't have stage fright, and this wasn't it. It was something else. It was this burning desire and hope.

Would Lance understand?

Ash's surroundings seemed to dim as they got lost in the song, but Lance stayed bright. Ash let Lance into their special musical world. It was a place that they saved only for themself, a place they never knew how to share. If Ash wasn't convinced before, the fact that Lance could penetrate this place proved he was special. This was important. This was a step that had to be taken to break down walls. Letting Lance into this space was the biggest thing Ash could offer.

And Lance understood. He watched Ash like he had watched them all night, but now he couldn't stop smiling.

Ash walked forward as they continued singing, each word becoming more intimate as they reached Lance. Ash held out a hand to his shoulder, and Lance grabbed their waist with both hands. Ash sat on his lap, trying to remember the words of the song instead of thinking about how close they were, instead of wanting to press closer and *feel* him like they never had. Then Ash let the last word ring out, and Lance stole the microphone. He set it down on an empty space on the

VALENTINE'S DAY TIGERS

bench. Their gazes locked then, unwavering, and Ash wondered if they would kiss for the first time. Because they were feeling it. Ash was really feeling it. Their legs trembled with the anticipation.

Lance's eyes darted to Ash's lips. He tilted his head and pressed his lips gently against theirs. He didn't push far. It was more of a whisper-kiss, but Ash didn't demand more. There was something about this that Lance was unsure about. Ash felt it too.

It was scary.

Having sex with a stranger, even an endearing stranger like Yuri, was nothing. This was everything. This was opening their heart to someone, becoming vulnerable.

It was about honesty.

Ash pulled away and said, "I met a Yuri last night. He was interesting and engaging, very forward, and sexy, and I didn't think you were coming back, Lance, and I just want to tell you now and apologize—"

Lance shut Ash up with a real kiss. He pressed his lips hard against theirs, and he bit at their lips like he was punishing them, begging them to stop. "I don't want to talk about that," he said. "I don't want to hear that. I know. And I don't need your apology. I'm not mad, Ash. I'm sorry for leaving without saying a word."

106

"You know? How?"

"Where I live, we had really bad cell reception, and I would have had to use our public landline to call you, so I never gave you a phone number." Lance shook his head.

"That's not what I—"

"But things have been changing, and that little town is becoming way more livable, not so prehistoric, and I'm ready to give you my number, Ash. I don't ever want to lose contact with you again." He lifted a hand and gently touched Ash's cheek. "I've been falling in love with you all this time. I love you, okay? I'll prove it."

He kissed Ash again. Ash instinctively parted their lips. They wanted some answers, but Lance was quickly making it hard to think about anything but him. He was good about sucking on their lower lip and driving them out of their mind, but he wouldn't take Ash's cue to dive in.

But *love*.

Lance loved them. He just said it, and he meant it. Ash knew him well enough to know that he would never have said it otherwise. Their chest felt full like their heart was growing several sizes and might explode right out of there.

VALENTINE'S DAY TIGERS

Ash buried their fingers in Lance's almost-white hair and said, "Let's go to my place."

CHAPTER 12

Y URI HAD NO IDEA where he was going. He just kept lumbering forward. His usually deft tiger paws were clumsy, and he kept dragging his head in the snow, trying to work through a throbbing brain and blurry vision. He was far from the Lodge and any of the cabins in Eurio. No one was following him. He had either lost the others or they had let him go, but none of that mattered at the moment. He was trying to figure out how to stop this pain.

He was over it. So over it.

Instead of just double everything, Yuri had entire visions play across his eyes. It was as if the dream he had last night overlaid all of reality. He almost didn't

VALENTINE'S DAY TIGERS

think it was real when he came across the same black and white spruces he had seen in his dream. Black and white spruces were nothing new, but this area was eerily familiar. It was darker. The trees were larger. The snow was blinding.

Yuri lifted his head and shook off the snow he had accumulated. It didn't work very well because he didn't shake for long. It hurt too much. He swore he could hear a reverberating rattle like his brain had been dislodged and was rolling around in his skull. Then the darkness shattered. If not for the stars, it would have been pitch-black; they were like needle-thin pin lights piercing through the snowy canopy.

He stopped moving and stared. No, those weren't lights. They weren't coming from above. They were right in front of him, coalescing into two shining sea-blue orbs. They were eyes.

Yuri took a step back. The low rumble of a growl came from that same direction, and he took another step back.

Before Yuri could whip around and run back the way he had come, a big silvery wolf jumped out of the shadows. Yuri was either really losing it or this was Luc Lenoir, the one who had made Yuri's life hell for so many years. Yuri wasn't a grudge holder exactly, but everything in his body was screaming and burning. He had never seen the shifter-witch hybrid in his wolf form before, but he knew. This wolf had a shimmery crescent mark on his forehead just like Luc. It was like the moon. Or, according to Trinity, the shifter alliance that treated the sun, earth, and moon like gods, the *Moon*.

Yuri growled and braced himself as the wolf ran. Yuri expected it to charge him. The wolf darted forward like a hurricane, whipping up snow and concealing himself in a blizzard of white. Yuri dug in his claws as it rushed at him, but nothing hard hit him. Only snow spattered his fur and fell away like harmless bits of dust.

Yuri wobbled as he turned, trying to catch sight of the wolf again. His claws dug deeper into the snow until they hit frigid earth.

This needed to stop.

He slowly unanchored his claws and walked around cautiously. There was no sign of the silvery wolf. It was as if he had disappeared in that flurry of snow.

Or he had never been there to begin with.

Yuri was known for jumping headfirst into things, but this was a game that had to be played differently—

VALENTINE'S DAY TIGERS

especially if it was real.

When Yuri crossed another line of spruces, the landscape changed. These large holes pocked the area as far as he could see. They could be dangerous, like landmines, if one wasn't paying attention.

Yuri stayed clear of them, he didn't need to get stuck in a hole on top of getting hunted by a big-ass wolf. Luc Lenoir was a monster. How big was that wolf? Much bigger than a Siberian tiger. Yuri wasn't used to that; he was a thousand pounds of deadly predator.

The crackling of a branch caught Yuri's attention. He sunk lower, belly against the snow, as he stalked forward. Then something barreled into his side. Sharp pain exploded in his ribs, and Yuri went flying. He landed on his side, skidded, and rolled in the snow. He extended his claws and found purchase on solid ground, but the snow sped him up too much. The back half of his body jerked down like he was getting sucked up into the earth. He slid farther and held tighter until his front claws were the only things stopping him from falling into one of those large holes. He gripped the ledge and put all his strength into his upper body to pull himself back up.

But the ledge crumbled.

He swiped at the air but caught nothing. For a few distorted seconds, he was weightless. Then his back hit icy dirt with a thud and a pop. His head throbbed worse than before. The seizure never came, but the pain paralyzed his body.

All he could think was this: Josh hadn't managed to get all the Black Magic out of his system. It was still in there, and it was still killing him because of Luc Lenoir.

But why did it take this long? He had been fine, perfect even, for over two weeks, ever since Josh left. Did he just delay the inevitable?

Yuri looked up—his eyes were the only things he could move. He expected the wolf to be circling the hole while staring down at him with hungry eyes, but there was nothing. Snow began to fall. Everything was silent as death. Eventually, the paralysis subsided, and Yuri almost wished it hadn't. He hadn't been aware of the fire licking his right foreleg, concentrated like lava in his shoulder. It was dislocated.

He gingerly got to his paws and limped around the bottom of the ditch. It was rather narrow and deep. He wasn't sure he'd be able to make the jump with one of his legs out of commission. He tried it anyway. He leaned back on his haunches and sprang forward. He caught the edge, but he couldn't pull himself up because his right foreleg bubbled fire, and he fell.

Yuri roared as he hit the frozen earth once again. He was missing small patches of fur from where he had gotten burned when he went out with Ash. They weren't bad and had healed a great deal; they were hardly noticeable in this form. But now they hurt too, as if they were brand new. Yuri was pretty good at withstanding pain, but he was about to reach his limit. It didn't help that he couldn't think with the constant pounding in his skull.

When it got this bad, Lance was the only thing that came to Yuri's mind. Most of the time, he was right there, so maybe it made sense. Lance was his security, but Yuri was alone. His brother wasn't here. Even when he was, Yuri always had to work through the pain on his own. He would overcome because he was stubborn and clung to life like no other. Hell, but he could have used his brother's help.

Yuri shook his head and limped around again. He went as far as he could until his backside was against a frozen dirt wall, and then he repeated the jump. He got farther this time. He clawed into the earth as he made his ruined shoulder work through pure force of will and dragged himself out. When all three of his working legs were planted safely on solid ground, he started hobbling home.

He didn't see any wolf tracks.

He didn't smell anything.

And he saw no sign of Luc.

Yuri clenched his jaw and kept his eyes forward. There were just a bunch of random holes out in the middle of the woods outside of the Toran Pack's usual territory. It was no big deal. It was nothing. It was all nothing. The pain was making him hallucinate. The ditch he fell into likely wasn't that deep. It was probably the only hole out there and his double vision had tricked him into thinking there had been more.

He just had to make it home. Everything would be fine when he made it home because Lance would be there.

CHAPTER 13

LANCE KNEW ASH WAS a wanderer, but he somehow hadn't expected them to be living in a hotel. It proved they never intended on staying long but had ended up doing just that. Was it because of him?

He looked the hotel room over. It was basic, but it was clean. Ash obviously didn't own much, just that ukulele and that big reddish truck parked outside.

And some cat food apparently.

"I know it's not much, but that's what happens when you jump from place to place," Ash said. "Just a second. Let me put out this food. I'm technically not supposed to, but I found some stray cats and couldn't help myself." Ash pumped their fist. "Rebel life."

Lance chuckled at that. Ash was too cute for this world. After grabbing the bag of cat food and a bowl, Ash gave Lance a friendly nudge with their elbow. "I'll be back," they said. But they didn't move. They stayed, leaning on their tiptoes. So, Lance kissed them, guessing that was what they wanted. And it was. Ash lingered there, pressing their body into him, trying to wrap their arms around him even though the bag and bowl made that impossible. All it took was one kiss, and the dam had come down. Ash had been waiting for Lance to invite them in.

That made him nervous.

"Okay. Now I'll really be back," Ash said.

"Get going already." Lance placed his hand on Ash's lower back and escorted them to the door.

"You're not trying to get rid of me, are you?"

"I'm trying to get you back in here as quick as possible."

Ash hummed. "I like the sound of that."

Lance opened the door for Ash, and they slipped through. They gestured for him to shut the door with exaggerated sweeps of their arms, since their hands were preoccupied, and then tiptoed down the hall. Apparently, they knew where the cameras were and how to avoid them because they were really getting away

VALENTINE'S DAY TIGERS

with this. Lance closed the door and shook his head. Of course Ash fed strays. That was so like them.

Maybe it was that big heart that had initially drawn him in. Or their voice. Or maybe everything about Ash—except for sexual attraction.

Lance cursed, took off his coat, hung it up, and proceeded to strip off his boots. Then he started snooping around, but there was nothing to see. It was just as he had assessed when walking into the room. Ash had next to nothing. He knew they were a minimalist, but this was extreme. At least he had seen odds and ends kept in their truck. It was Ash's real home.

When Ash came back, Lance said, "You've stayed here for a while, huh? People don't usually stay in a hotel long."

"Very true," Ash agreed. "I didn't plan on staying this long, but I don't plan on much." Ash took off their boots and hung up their coat. "You can sit somewhere, you know? The bed. That chair. Whatever."

Lance didn't move. He studied Ash, doing his best to read them. He wondered what he should say. He knew what he needed to do. Sort of. He had to prove his love, and then he'd get to keep Ash, right? How was he supposed to do that, though? Was he supposed to bring up sex or would Ash? What was the right thing to

118

do here? He knew they wanted it, based on their scent, but...

"Lance."

"Ash."

"You're staring."

"Uh, yep. It's your rainbow hair. I never get tired of staring at it."

Ash snorted. "Just my hair, huh?" They tugged at Lance's shirt. "You kissed me for the first time today, and all I can think about is kissing you again and again." Their eyes glimmered like emeralds as they walked their fingers up Lance's chest and to the back of his neck, where Ash hooked their hand. "Stay with me tonight?"

Well, that answered his question, didn't it? Ash wanted sex, loud and clear. They often gave off an intense wave of sweet arousal, more so as Lance and Ash started unofficially seeing each other, even more when Lance finally kissed them.

Ash reached up with their other hand, applying pressure to the back of Lance's neck and urging him to bend down to meet them. He did, and their noses touched. Ash's eyelids grew heavy.

"I want to pick up where we left off at the karaoke bar," Ash said. They closed their eyes and moved their

VALENTINE'S DAY TIGERS

hips forward. They wanted to feel him. Lance liked being close to Ash. He wouldn't mind holding them one bit, but sex… sex made him so fucking nervous.

Lance tilted his head so he could capture Ash's lips with his. It was more of the same, soft caresses. But his mouth was parted slightly, and Ash took the opportunity to go deeper. They pressed their tongue against his teeth, and he opened his mouth a little wider at the request. He liked kissing fine until it involved too much tongue. Luckily, Ash didn't dart their tongue down his throat. They kept it shallow, inviting his tongue to dance along. He did his best, but it wasn't his favorite thing. And he sure as hell wasn't good at it.

Focus, he told himself.

He pulled back and asked, "Condom?"

"That can wait," Ash replied. They kissed Lance again, as deeply as he would let them. And it was pretty deep. He let Ash take total control since they seemed to know what they were doing and certainly knew what they wanted. Much more than Drew did. Drew hadn't had much experience, but Ash did. The difference was as clear as the lack of sun in an Alaskan winter.

Lance slid his hand down Ash's rib cage and rested it on their hip. Ash jerked back.

"Sorry," Lance said. He didn't know what he did

so terribly wrong already, but his heart was ready to bail and leave him alone with his embarrassment.

Ash clicked their tongue against the back of their teeth and said, "It wasn't you. You just touched the worst of my burns…"

"Burns?"

"I did something reckless last night, but it's fine. It's not bad."

Lance had said he didn't want to hear about Yuri last night. Now he wasn't so sure, but Ash didn't give him the opportunity to demand an explanation. They kissed him again and started fiddling with his clothes. "Way too many layers here."

Lance supposed he'd let the Yuri thing rest for now. It was done and in the past anyway. He needed to catch Ash's attention now. He needed Ash focused on him, and he had to prove his love was true.

Lance worked at his long-sleeved shirt first. He found it awkward to strip in front of Ash while they were staring so intently at him. It wasn't that he stumbled or anything, but that look in their eyes, the heat, the slight tremble in their legs, he couldn't help but think they were expecting way more than they were going to get. But that smile. He would die to see that smile every day.

VALENTINE'S DAY TIGERS

Not for the first time, he wondered if sex was that important. Did it mean that much? Was it the difference between really loving someone and not?

Ash reached out and touched his bare chest. So, he stopped. He would let Ash feel him out before getting to his pants. Their fingers lingered on his tattoos, tracing the lines that made them up. Their touch made him shiver a little, but it didn't arouse him.

C'mon, he thought.

"You have a lot of tattoos," Ash said.

"I guess you haven't seen me without a shirt before."

"Nope. Are their stories behind them?"

"Do they have to have stories?"

"There's always a story behind everything, no matter how small."

"I got tattoos with my brother and one of our close friends. It was kind of a thing we did for a while there."

"See? A story."

Ash let their hand linger when they placed their palm flat against the left side of Lance's chest. Ash seemed content to feel his heartbeat. Lance was too, but the longer they stayed like that, the more nervous he got for anything beyond this because he wasn't excited.

At last, Ash moved back to remove their crocheted sweater. The first things to catch Lance's eyes were the little blotches of burned red skin marring the even brown tone he had imagined seeing. His hand hovered above one. He almost touched it, but he didn't want to aggravate it any more. So, he grabbed a space on Ash's waist clear of the tiny burns and held fast as he asked, "Seriously, what the hell happened?" These were fresh burns, definitely from *last night*.

"I went on a little adventure out in the middle of nowhere." Ash dipped their chin to avoid eye contact. "They aren't bad. I promise. They've already faded a lot thanks to the aloe I put on them after I got back here."

Lance stiffened.

Yeah, the burns weren't bad, but what the fuck did Yuri take Ash out to do? Was he into kinky sex? Lance couldn't fathom what that would entail. What if he had gotten Ash seriously hurt? Lance was speechless and frozen. His head was spinning. His breaths came in faster and shorter.

"I'm gonna kill him," Lance growled. "After all this time, I'm going to be what kills him."

"What?" Ash frowned.

Lance scrubbed a hand down his face. Then he reached for the back of Ash's head and gripped their

VALENTINE'S DAY TIGERS

curly hair tightly enough so he could maneuver their head, but not so tightly it would hurt. He angled Ash's head up so they had to look at him.

"You ran off with my brother last night. That Yuri? That was my Yuri," Lance said.

Ash's jaw dropped. "You've got to be shitting me." They bit their lower lip. Then they grabbed Lance's waist, nails digging into his skin as if they were expecting him to become intangible. "Were you there? Were you there last night at Tipsy? You didn't say anything. I didn't see you. I wouldn't have… Lance."

"I'm not mad at you, Ash," Lance reminded.

"I wouldn't have done it, Lance," Ash insisted. "I thought you weren't coming back." Their fingers trembled against his skin. Lance hugged them to stop it. They were both topless, and it felt good to have Ash's skin pressed against his. It was the best kind of warmth; it was safe. It didn't make Lance feel vulnerable because it was so safe.

Ash clawed at his back and sniffled. "I feel so stupid. I thought you weren't coming back, that you didn't feel the same way, so I… I've never felt this way about anyone before. But you came back to me today. You came back."

Didn't feel the same way. Wasn't coming back, Lance

echoed.

Lance took a deep breath. "I know Yuri's got enough charm for ten people. Nobody knows how to resist him."

"It wasn't that." Ash choked out a laugh. "He screwed up his pick-up line big time. He was sure I'd say no after that and kept rolling with the punches, but I just… I didn't care how it might turn out." Ash swallowed. "I was in a bad place, okay? And spending the night with Yuri was crazy, every moment of it, but he did something for me. Something good. I wouldn't have gone to the library today, hoping to find you, if I hadn't almost been burned alive last night. If I hadn't conquered fire."

Lance let out a measured breath. "What kind of bad place?"

Ash rested their forehead against Lance's chest. "An I-don't-care-what-happens kind of bad place. It's been a long and lonely road. I've always gone where the wind takes me, and it never mattered where or what happened. Then I met you, and I stayed for you. So, maybe I betrayed you because of what I did last night, but if I hadn't done it, I wouldn't be with you now. I would be gone.

"Yuri made me realize what I wanted and that I

had to go for it, give it one more shot. I don't think what I've been doing all my life has been living. I've been watching everyone else instead. Well, no more. I want to be with you. I want to let you in. I want to live."

"I—what? Banging *Yuri* made you realize you want to be with *me*?" Lance asked incredulously. That didn't add up.

If tonight was a bust and Ash saw how broken Lance was, they would go back to Yuri in a heartbeat. He knew how this worked. Yuri would leave him and take Ash too. Yuri was interested in Ash. He said he wanted to go back and see them again, and that was bad news. That meant that last night went well, right? *Somehow.* It didn't sound like it went well to Lance, but what did he know? He didn't have anything on his brother. He had to change, and he had to make tonight good. *Really* good. He would always be a shadow, but maybe he could become more substantial.

Lance closed his eyes and concentrated on Ash's skin to remind himself that *he* was here with Ash, right now.

He almost wished Yuri would get sick again so that the rules would switch, so Yuri would need him again and not the other way around.

Lance's jaw clenched. *That's a fucking horrible*

thought, shithead.

"It's only been you for me, Lance," Ash said, breaking into his mind. "I'm sorry. I really am. Please, don't leave. I don't know how to make this up to you, but I want to try. I don't want to lose you. Every date, every moment I spend with you, all the time it took thawing the ice around us, it's been everything. It's made me feel something music can't. Before you, there was nothing but music for me. I perform in front of audiences, but I've always been alone until you. I can share my music space with you. That's the most precious thing I have. I… I love you, too."

How? How was Ash so perfect? How could they say things like this before they'd even had sex, like Lance was their mate and therefore someone they couldn't lose? Could it be true? Or would it all fall apart like it did with Drew?

"Ash," Lance said. He gently cupped their cheek. "I'm not mad, okay? You had every reason to doubt me. You had every reason to think I wouldn't be coming back. And *I'm* sorry. I'm trying to fix it now. You were right to doubt me because I almost didn't come back, but it's not for the reason you think. It's not because I don't feel the same way." He hoped like hell that wasn't a lie.

VALENTINE'S DAY TIGERS

Ash waited, searching his eyes. They probably wanted Lance to give a better explanation than that, but he didn't. He couldn't.

"You came back, and that has to mean something. When you said you love me, that has to mean something."

"It does. I mean it," Lance said.

"I love you too, Lance."

The sweet scent of Ash's arousal was as strong as ever, so Lance knew he hadn't ruined things beyond repair yet. "Do you still want me to spend the night?"

"Uhm, yes. Very much yes."

"Your burns really don't hurt?"

"Nah, just watch out for that one spot if you're worried." As if to prove Ash's point, they took Lance's hand and guided his palm down their side and then back up to cup their breasts, one and then the other. Ash's nipples got hard at the same time their arousal became as sweet as cotton candy.

Lance was down to sleep with Ash—sex not so much—but he had to. He couldn't be so fucking pathetic forever, not if he wanted to keep Ash. There was no more time to waste for any of it. He had hurt Ash by keeping them at a safe distance from his heart. Yuri was better now and he was going to leave. Lance needed to step up and take control or his life would be left in tatters.

Ash touched Lance's lips. "Thank you for giving me another chance."

"Another chance? We're just picking up where we left off." Lance took their hand and kissed it.

Ash kissed his chest, right over his pounding heart. "Shall we continue, then?"

"Yes."

No.

CHAPTER 14

ASH AND LANCE WORKED on their pants and underwear at the same time. Ash was so turned on; their arousal was dripping down their thighs. They squeezed their legs together and then looked at Lance. He hated that their eyes went right to his soft dick.

"One of us is way hornier than the other," Ash said.

Lance laughed because it was either that or panic, and he was already on the verge of panic. "Talking about my brother ruined the mood."

"Then we're going to have to fix that." Ash brushed their fingers down Lance's thighs. "How do you have so much muscle? What's your gym routine like?"

"Don't like it?"

"You're sexy as hell, Lance. Sexier than I could've ever imagined."

Well, Lance supposed that was points for him. At least Ash liked his body.

Ash pressed their hand against his stomach and trailed fingers down his happy trail. It made his skin jump, but he forced himself to stay still and gritted his teeth as Ash explored him. They ran their hand down his shaft, gently squeezed his balls, and went back to his shaft, coaxing his dick to attention effortlessly. The whole time they did it, he made sure to think about sex, about being aroused. He stared down at Ash's nipples and tried to conjure up every erotic thought he could, anything to get his brain and body online for what was about to happen. Luckily, his body was getting the memo. The stimulation Ash provided helped big time.

Okay. I can do this, he thought.

Ash looked up at him. "Better?"

He nodded, because he was afraid if he spoke, he would say something wrong.

"You seem a little stiff." Ash poked his left shoulder. Their finger lingered on his arm as they traced the

VALENTINE'S DAY TIGERS

white tiger face he had tattooed there.

"Too excited," Lance gritted out.

"Well, try to relax a little." Ash ran their hands down his arms and sides, and it helped. Ash felt good. This warmth, these soft caresses. Just like Drew, Ash wanted Lance to enjoy this. So, he had to. He couldn't let them down. And he needed to make sure Ash got everything they wanted.

"How do you want me to touch you? Show me." Lance said.

Ash laughed, green eyes twinkling. "Have you never done this before, or do I just make you that nervous?"

"Kind of both."

"How can it be 'kind of both'?"

"Last time I did this it was with another guy," Lance said, though he omitted how long it had been since then, and that he had only done it once.

"Got it." Ash took Lance's hand and mapped out their body for him. "I really like your hands on my lower back." Lance rested a hand there, just above their ass. Ash arched their back in response and let out a little moan.

"Of course, breasts and vagina like love too."

Ash dropped one of their hands in between their

legs and started rubbing. Lance watched carefully and noticed the way Ash seemed to melt into vulnerability.

Lance followed Ash's hand and moved it away to cup their sex with his own hand. He thought Ash had reacted strongly before, but it was nothing compared to now. They rolled their hips forward and against his hand.

"Yes," they said.

Lance tried to ignore the sticky liquid coating his fingers and the potent smell that accosted his nose like a tickle that wouldn't go away. Whenever he jerked off, he made sure to do it in the shower because he hated the mess. The look on Ash's face meant they were enjoying this immensely, so he pushed the discomfort aside. He touched different areas and did more of the same when Ash reacted well and when they verbally told him to keep doing that. He dipped one finger inside of them, and the rocking of Ash's hips intensified.

"My legs are gonna give out," Ash said. It was then Lance noticed their legs shaking. "Meet you on the bed? You can get that condom."

Lance nodded, and Ash stumbled to the bed. Lance tried to ignore the need to wipe off the remnants of arousal on his fingers, but he ended up doing it anyway, against his thigh—though that didn't exactly make

VALENTINE'S DAY TIGERS

him feel better—when Ash had their back turned, and he used his unsullied hand to grab that condom out of his wallet. Putting it on was awkward as hell because his hands were shaking. However, he was pleased to see that he was fully hard. His body understood what would be happening next, brain too. He'd perform.

When he was ready, he went to Ash, who was lying back-first on the bed with their knees in the air and legs wide. A red flush spread across their chest, and their fingers were at their sex again, rubbing and dipping inside as Lance had done. He worried Ash was doing this because he hadn't done it well enough. But when he got on the bed and crawled over to them, they opened their eyes and smiled wide.

Ash grabbed the back of Lance's head and pulled him in for a lingering kiss. Lance tried to ignore the fact that sex was messy and kissed Ash back. Ash was fierce, and they introduced rolling hips like they were on a loop. Ash hit him in a sensitive spot, and Lance lost his breath for a moment.

"Ready?" Ash asked.

"Ready." Lance was pretty sure he had never told a bigger lie in his life.

Ash took his length in hand. He was hyperaware, almost to extreme discomfort, of every touch, but he followed Ash as they slowly positioned him where they needed. He lowered his hips more and gently pushed. Ash let out a long moan and said, "Do it again."

So, Lance did, and he buried himself deeper this time. There wasn't much resistance because of how wet Ash was, but they were tight, and Lance was feeling it now. His breaths came quicker. Ash told him to move.

He met Ash's wild hips with his own and pushed himself inside, balls deep. Ash clawed at his hair as they whimpered his name, begging him for more. So, he moved a bit faster. Thankfully, he didn't have to think too much about it because his mind and body were at the point they knew exactly what needed to be done to reach a much-needed release. Stimulation and pressure in just the right areas… and then Ash crashed around him. The rhythmic pulses of their body coaxed him to come too, in one big burst.

Hell, it was a relief. He didn't know how much longer he could stand that buzz of arousal. He was glad to let it go.

He continued to hold himself up with his arms as he rode out the rest of their orgasms. And then, like that, it was over and done. He couldn't help thinking he just wanted to take a shower to get all the crud off him. He'd take Ash with him, wash them too. But he

VALENTINE'S DAY TIGERS

pushed those thoughts away and stayed still. He watched Ash's chest rise and fall as they slowly came down from climax.

Finally, Ash opened their eyes; they twinkled like fucking stars. Their smile glowed soft like candlelight. Lance had never seen Ash more satisfied. Never. And he didn't understand it. Ash looked like they had just experienced the best moment of their life, like they were just coming down from heaven, but he didn't think this was any better than jerking off alone—except for seeing Ash's satisfaction. That was much better.

Lance worked off the condom and tossed it in the trash.

You did it, he told himself. *You did it.*

CHAPTER 15

LANCE SIGHED AND RAN his hand through his hair. There were sticky clumps in it. He tried to ignore them and lay down beside Ash. Ash cuddled into his side, hips still gyrating. He moved back subtly when Ash hit too-sensitive nerve endings. He really didn't want to be touched again so soon after orgasm. Other places were fine, but anything "erotic" was too much. Luckily, Ash didn't seem to notice or mind. They smiled and buried their face into his chest.

"Good?" Lance asked. Maybe he shouldn't have. Maybe that wasn't something normal people asked after sex. He didn't really know. He didn't know much about sex. Not even porn. It never interested him

VALENTINE'S DAY TIGERS

much.

"Good?" Ash repeated. They shifted so they could look Lance in the eye. "Hell yeah, it was good. Wasn't it good for you?"

"Of course. The best." Lance tried to smile, but he didn't feel it. In fact, he felt something much different, something that made his lips quiver.

"Lance," Ash touched his cheek, "what's wrong?"

Lance clenched his jaw as he remembered Drew's harsh words: *"Don't lie. You don't love me."*

"Nothing's wrong," he said.

"Hey." Ash kissed his lips softly, sweetly. "Look at me."

Lance hadn't realized he had started to look away, but he forced himself to obey.

"Tell me the truth. Something is obviously wrong. You look like you're about to cry."

Great. That was worse than anything. Lance wasn't even a crier by nature, so what was this shit?

"You came out to see me tonight. You said you almost didn't come back, but not for the reason I think. So, what does that mean? What is all of this about?"

Lance refused to close his eyes and shut out all visual stimulus. "I love you, Ash. I really do, but I tried to ignore it and never admitted it to myself because I was sure it would never go anywhere. But every time I saw you, my heart would race. Every time you touched me, every time our eyes met, all of it."

Ash gave that same glowing smile. "I feel that too. It's something magical. Romantic, I guess. I'm new to this." Ash touched his chest again, just over his heart. And Lance's heart beat a little faster like it always did. That hadn't changed. Ash gave him butterflies.

"I just… When I tell you the truth, Ash, don't say I don't love you." Lance said, practically begging. Was he really doing this? Was this smart?

Ash furrowed their normally smooth as butter brow in confusion, but they waited for him to say more.

"I do love you. I wouldn't be here doing this if I didn't. I also wouldn't be so mad at my brother about last night." It was then Lance realized he understood exactly how Austin felt when Mateo was out doing dangerous things with him and Yuri. This had to be love. He truly did understand it, and that was why he hated seeing those two together sometimes. He joked and said they were disgusting, but that wasn't true. He felt the same way about Ash. He swore he did. Just not about sex. He never wanted to admit these feelings even to himself because he was going to lose. He knew

VALENTINE'S DAY TIGERS

he was going to lose Ash. He could feel it coming with his next words: the truth.

"I don't understand," Ash whispered.

"I don't feel this," Lance confessed. "I don't get what's so great about sex. I'd be just as happy to have a romantic dinner with you or to cuddle on the couch while watching a movie with you. Actually, I would like that a lot more." He bit his lower lip. "I'm sorry." His eyes burned like hell. "I don't know why I'm fucked-up like this."

Ash sat up suddenly. "No way." They took Lance's arm and tugged. He sat up too. It was hard to look Ash in the eye, but he made himself do it. God, he was ashamed.

"Mark my words, Lance. There is nothing wrong with you. There's nothing wrong with feeling that way. I'm not mad, and I don't think any less of you." Ash wiped away a tear that had managed to escape Lance's eye. "Would you say you're asexual, then?"

"Yeah, I guess."

"There's *nothing* wrong with that."

"Other than I have no idea how to satisfy a lover who feels differently, so why would you want to stay with me?"

"I may not be asexual, but I get being different

You know, I'm non-binary. You aren't obligated to have sex, Lance. So get that idea out of your head right now. And don't think it's a deal-breaker for me. It wasn't sex that made me fall in love with you. I won't lie and say I didn't enjoy what we did just now. It meant a lot to me, but if you never want to do it again, I won't hold it against you, okay?"

"I don't believe that," Lance said.

Ash put their pointer finger to his lip. "Then *I'll* have to prove it. But don't run away from me because you don't think I'll be happy. That's not for you to decide."

He wondered.

Ash pulled Lance in and hugged him. "I love you, Lance. I do. And you're the first person I've ever said that to, so I hope you know how much that means."

Lance's cell phone went off. He wanted to revel in Ash's words. He wanted to hold on to them to keep them from leaving him, but he knew that ringtone. He gave Ash a quick squeeze before jumping off the bed and fishing his phone out of his pants pocket.

"Yuri," he said in a flat tone.

"Lance, I need you to fix my shoulder. I'm doing a shitty job of it on my own. It's dislocated."

Lance growled. "Tell Mateo to do it. You're out

VALENTINE'S DAY TIGERS

with him right now, right? You must have managed to drag him away from Austin for once. If anyone could, it'd be you. He always took things plenty far, but even he had some sense of when to stop. He probably warned you."

"I'm not out with Mateo." There was something weird in Yuri's voice. Lance couldn't say what it was exactly, but he knew his brother, and the rich tones that usually made up his voice were missing. His voice was hollow.

"Are you okay?" Lance asked.

Yuri hesitated. "No."

And Lance was ready to go. When Yuri said he wasn't okay, he meant it.

"I'll call you back," Lance said as he crushed the phone between his shoulder and ear and worked to get his underwear and pants on. So much for that shower.

Lance hung up and turned to Ash. "I have to go."

"Okay." Ash stared at him, wide-eyed.

"I'll be back."

Lance leaned down to kiss Ash. He hated the hesitation on Ash's lips as they kissed him back, as if they were wondering if it was okay to kiss him. But he couldn't figure it out now or fix the damage he had dealt. Yuri needed him.

"Wait for me," Lance said.

"I'll wait. Go to your brother."

Once Lance had all of his things, and he and Ash had exchanged phone numbers, he hurried out the door as millions of little claws pricked his skin and threatened to tear him apart.

Yeah, they had exchanged phone numbers, but he had probably ruined everything.

CHAPTER 16

ONE MORE TIME YURI tried popping his right shoulder back into its socket. He was strong, but with the pain coursing through his body, he just couldn't get it right. Not to mention the angle was all wrong. He had jarred his arm worse by this point and was ready to give up until Lance got home.

Lance was taking way too fucking long, though. Yuri could've had this taken care of by now if he went to anybody else in Eurio, but he needed Lance.

What the hell was Lance doing all the way in Fairbanks anyway? That was where he had confirmed he was on the phone.

Sweat poured down Yuri's forehead as he sat

down and tried to stop moving his arm. He wanted to lie down, but that hurt too much. He wiped away the sweat with his good hand and was relieved to hear the familiar rumble of an engine stalling at the front of the cabin. A few moments later, Lance walked in through the door.

"About time you got here," Yuri said. He smirked, but another twinge of pain stopped the expression from lasting very long.

He had managed to pull on some pants since returning to the cabin, but that was it. Because of that, Lance could take a good look at him. He stared at Yuri's right shoulder and didn't say a word. He stormed forward, grabbed Yuri forcefully, and shoved him down onto the ground none too gently. Yuri's shoulder screamed, and he screamed along with it as Lance popped it back into the socket. It hurt like a motherfucker, but then it felt better. A lot better. It would be sore for a little while, but at least it could heal properly now.

Lance got off him and held out his hand. Yuri took it, with his left, and Lance pulled him to his feet.

"Thanks, Lance."

"Why did you wait so long to get that taken care of?"

VALENTINE'S DAY TIGERS

"I tried to do it on my own, but I just couldn't get it right."

"No shit. You fucked it up more." Lance touched Yuri's forehead. "You're hot. Are you feeling okay? What's going on? What were you doing?"

Yuri didn't want to talk about any of that. They were extraneous details that didn't have anything to do with anything. None of what happened was real. Yuri was just having a relapse. He didn't like it, but Lance would take it much worse. Lance was the one who dwelled on stuff, not him. He had no idea what was going on, but he was going to choose to ignore it, to move on, because it had no place in his life.

It wasn't real.

"You smell like sex," Yuri commented, because Lance did. Big time.

Lance moved his ice-like eyes to the burns on Yuri's skin, and then there was a burst of red. He cracked Yuri across the face with his fist.

Yuri stumbled back and caught himself on the couch's wooden arm. "Fuck!" he shouted. "What was that for?"

"What were you thinking last night? You took Ash out into the middle of nowhere to get hypothermia and burned and shit?" Lance demanded. "You haven't been better that long and you're back to being as reckless as you were when you thought this was all going to end with you dying from those seizures."

Yuri rubbed his jaw and wiped away a trickle of blood. "I never stopped being reckless."

"No fucking joke, but I thought you were learning to tone it down a little bit. I thought I understood why you did it. Because you didn't know how long your future would be, you wanted to live every moment and be normal. Is that wrong? What about now? You're fully healed! Was last night necessary? Do you want to die?"

"You're starting to sound like Gale."

"We have things to lose now, Yuri, and we have everything to gain."

Lance was trying to sound positive or something, but Yuri saw the way his jaw twitched. This time he was ready when Lance launched himself at him. He darted out of the way and Lance collided with the couch, toppling it over with a crack. Then Lance was back on his feet, coming at Yuri again. Yuri caught him this time, but his shoulder protested that move. Lance got the better of him and shoved him against a wall. Yuri kneed him in the stomach. Lance crumpled long enough for Yuri to put some space between them.

VALENTINE'S DAY TIGERS

Then Lance was back on him, and this time his eyes were flickering to his animal. So Yuri beat him to it. He called to his tiger half and started shifting. He barely pulled off his pants in time to save them from being shredded as his bones popped and skin morphed. When he was finished, he was staring at a mirror image of himself. The only difference was that the tiger in front of him was white with eyes so light blue they were almost red.

Their tails cracked like whips. Anything standing on the entertainment set or the coffee table had no chance. Lance didn't even seem to care about that new TV he spent hours searching for—because he just *had* to find the right one, just like they *had* to have the best generator—as he rushed forward, jumped over it, and smacked it with his tail to get a swipe at Yuri. Yuri almost dodged, but Lance caught Yuri's tail between his teeth. Yuri roared his displeasure as he spun around and scratched Lance across the face. It was a deep cut, and he narrowly missed his brother's right eye. It was too damn close.

But Lance kept coming.

Yuri held back this time. He let it happen because maybe all Lance needed was one more good hit on him. Yuri grimaced when Lance jumped and clawed him and the curtains as Lance almost forced them both out the window. Luckily the twins missed hitting it head-on, so the glass stayed intact, but the wall rumbled, and the wood squeaked underneath their weight.

Enough was enough. Their cabin was going to be totally wrecked by the time they were done. And Lance didn't stop with one more hit. He got in several good slashes, so Yuri kicked him off with his hind legs. They tumbled across the floor as claws flew and blood followed. They grappled like that, one on top and then the other, neither of them gaining ground, until Yuri finally managed to push through the pain of his right foreleg and pinned Lance down for good. He made sure to trap all four of Lance's legs as he practically lay on top of him. Lance needed to stop moving already. Each time he struggled, Yuri flinched, but his willpower was greater than the physical pain.

The two of them growled in each other's faces, long canines threatening to tear flesh, but neither of them lashed out again. Their only options now were to go for faces and necks. It seemed that was enough to knock some sense into Lance. He started shifting. That usually meant he was done. Yuri gladly followed him, though he made sure to keep the upper hand. He wasn't going to let his brother out from underneath him until

VALENTINE'S DAY TIGERS

he was sure this temper tantrum had run its course.

"Are you finished?" Yuri asked, chest heaving. "Don't answer that. You are. We're done. No more fighting."

Blood from a cut along Yuri's jaw dripped onto Lance's face. Lance winced, but his teeth were bared, and his eyes were burning red. He wasn't finished yet.

CHAPTER 17

"WHEN YOU GET LIKE this, I know you need to talk," Yuri said. "So, talk."

Lance wiped Yuri's blood from his cheek along with the blood from his own cut lip. He trembled, and his eyes glinted red to blue to red, so Yuri held tighter. He wasn't in the mood for another fistfight, and his right shoulder was screaming at him again, but it wasn't like he had much of a choice. It was better to keep Lance in a bind than to have him wailing on Yuri. It was less painful.

"Just the two of us," Yuri said. "It's always been just the two of us. That's why I didn't ask anybody else for help, okay?" He wasn't sure if this was what Lance wanted to hear, but he had to try. He hadn't answered Lance's questions earlier, so maybe it would help. "Mateo came and went, but we are never going anywhere. We made that promise when Dad died, and that's the one constant I count on, Lance. That's why you had to be the one to fix my shoulder. No one else was around when I did it, and I didn't even think about anybody else. I called you. When you said you were on your way back, I was going to wait."

Lance started laughing. "Oh, really? It's just the two of us? You count on me? You're going to wait for *me*? What about all the times you've run off and done crazy shit on your own when even Mateo wouldn't go along with you or even before that when it was just me and I said it was too much? Or what about when we were sixteen and we hot-wired an SUV so we could go to Fairbanks whenever we wanted just so *you* could play around, flirt, and get laid?"

"What the fuck are you trying to say, Lance? You were right there with me."

"I followed you because that's what I've done my entire life! I'm a shadow. I always follow you, Yuri. I can't escape you."

"What?"

"And then you went and tried to steal Ash from

me! You were always going to leave me. As soon as Josh cured your PWD, it was just a matter of time."

"Stole Ash?"

"I met Ash months ago while I was trying to figure out a way to save you."

Little pieces of a puzzle Yuri didn't know he needed to solve began falling into place. "That's why you started spending so much time in Fairbanks," he said. "Sounds like you're the one who's going to leave me. Not the other way around."

"That's what you don't get! I can't do it!" Lance screamed. "I'm not good at sex like you are. No one's ever going to want me."

Yuri stared down at his brother, perplexed. "Good at it? It's not hard. And what does sex have to do with somebody wanting you? I want you. You're my brother."

"It's not the same. Look at Austin and Mateo. I want something like that with Ash. And sex *is* hard when you don't particularly like it."

And then more pieces of the puzzle fell into place. "You love Ash," Yuri said. "All this time you've been accusing Mateo and Austin of being gross. You hypocrite." Lance's gaze flickered, but Yuri grabbed his chin. "Look at me."

VALENTINE'S DAY TIGERS

"You never knew," Lance said. His lips quivered and he pressed them together for a moment to make it stop. "We were sixteen, and you were experimenting, and we spent so much time out in Fairbanks. We were always going out. You thought I was doing the same thing as you, right?"

"Well, yeah."

"I wasn't. I found someone I latched onto, someone I liked a lot, and I never told you because of our promise. I loved him. I met up with him every time you and I split up. He was always there, and then one day he wanted to experiment, have sex, because he was attracted to me. I went along with it, but I wasn't attracted to him. I'm not sexually attracted to anybody, and I hurt him that night because of that. I never saw him again."

Yuri's grip on Lance's chin tightened. "Really?"

"Yes, really," Lance growled. "You could have anybody you want, but you don't want to stay with anyone. Why?"

So, Lance wanted a heart-to-heart talk. It wasn't Yuri's favorite thing, but he'd do it for his brother, no questions asked. "I tried dating back then too. I didn't like it. Most of the girls I met were too boring, and I especially hated dinner dates where they'd stare into your eyes like they were waiting for some sort of magic to happen, or like they felt some sort of magic. You know, that sparkle, that lingering look that Mateo and Austin share. Weston and Cary. Gale and Cedar... I could go on, but I don't get it. And I don't like it. Especially holding hands, casual kissing, and cuddling. It's not my thing."

Lance laughed again, but it was interrupted by a hiccup. He closed his eyes shut tight. "We're opposites on everything, aren't we?"

"Maybe, but I guess that's why we work so well together."

Lance sighed. At last, all the fire left his system.

"We should get up and get washed off," Yuri said. "Also, our cabin looks like the aftermath of a shitstorm."

Lance frowned. "This sucks." He craned his neck and looked at the demolished TV. Then he winced. "Super sucks."

Yuri got up, unpinning his brother, and held out his hand. Lance took it, allowing him to tug Lance to his feet. The two of them went to the bathroom first, where Yuri took care of his wounds in front of the mirror as Lance hopped into the shower. Once Lance was out, Yuri was comfortably dressed, and his wounds

VALENTINE'S DAY TIGERS

were taken care of as well as they needed to be. Yuri took out some peroxide and put it on a cotton ball and pressed it against the deep cuts on Lance's cheek.

Lance hissed. "Fuck. Stop it. I can take care of it myself."

Yuri smirked. "I know. I'm just vindictive."

He left Lance to it and assessed the damage in the living room. Lance's precious TV was seriously done for. The screen was cracked. The couch was in tatters too. It had somehow gotten broken in half during that whole fiasco. The curtains had to go. The coffee table and Lance's computer looked intact, though. Any fragile odds and ends either made it or didn't. At least they didn't have much in the room these days, or in the rest of the cabin for that matter. Yuri started breaking down the things that needed to go and went from there.

Lance joined him eventually. "Sorry for freaking out."

"Whatever." Yuri playfully punched his brother in the arm. "And get those stupid thoughts out of your head. I'm not going to up and leave you one day. I don't want a mate anyway."

Yuri was no dummy. He knew that most people and shifters longed for a mate, but he also knew that he didn't, and he accepted that. It didn't bother him. In fact, he was quite content.

Or he had been.

"But you do," Yuri said. "Hell, and if you really don't like sex, Ash must be something special for you to want them so badly that you'd go and do it."

Yuri absentmindedly fingered a burn that he had gotten on his little romp with Lance's lover. He liked Ash too. Ash was interesting, someone he wouldn't mind sticking around. Also, he wouldn't mind fucking them again. "I'm sorry, though," Yuri said. "I wouldn't have taken Ash out if I had known how you feel."

"I'm not mad about the sex," Lance said. "It doesn't bother me at all, actually." He paused. Then his eyes lit up. "I have a crazy idea. What if we brought Ash in, sort of like we did Mateo."

"You mean tried to," Yuri corrected. "He did that whole leaving thing you were talking about."

"He didn't really, though. I know we keep saying that, but he'd still come running if we needed him."

"Yeah, probably."

"Mateo isn't close anymore, but he's our brother. Things change, but that doesn't. That won't. Bringing Ash in would change things too, but it would be good."

"Change," Yuri repeated. It never bothered him

VALENTINE'S DAY TIGERS

before, but he had also never thought that Lance would be at the forefront of it.

"You like Ash, right?" Lance asked.

Yuri shrugged. "Yeah."

"You even talked about seeing them again."

"Yeah, I did."

"Like a date?"

"No. Didn't I just tell you that I don't like dates? I wanted to hear them sing, and I wanted to take them out for trouble again."

"Ash likes dates," Lance said. "Ash... Ash is perfect."

Yuri waited for Lance to say something else. But he started staring off into space. He got the same dumb look on his face that Mateo and Austin did when they stared at each other. Gale and Cedar. Weston and Cary. Mates, mates, mates, mates.

"And?" Yuri coaxed.

Lance's eyes widened, and then he shook his head like he just realized he had frozen up. "We can all have what we want."

"Which is?"

"To stay together."

"Lance."

"I don't want to let Ash go, but I don't want to let

1 5 8

you go either. You're my brother, Yuri, and you always will be. It's always been the two of us. We'll always have each other's backs, and I have no intention of leaving you alone. I wouldn't do that to you. I… I'm sorry I thought you'd do that to me."

"I'm not going to die if you leave with Ash," Yuri said. But he also didn't say how much it would hurt. Lance was his closest person in this world, and it would hurt like hell if he left.

"That's what I was trying to say. Ash and I like dates, and romance, and cuddling, and staring into each other's eyes. I don't like sex, but Ash likes sex. *You* like sex."

"Hell no. You're not bringing me into your love life. If you and Ash are going to be a thing, if they're going to be your mate, it has to be because of *you*."

"Wrong. We're a package deal. And you like Ash. You said so."

"You're being ridiculous."

"Am I?"

"If Ash loves you, they'll accept you, all of you, or else they don't deserve you. Okay? Besides, you're not broken, Lance, no matter what you've been telling yourself all these years."

Lance frowned. "Does that mean you don't want

VALENTINE'S DAY TIGERS

Ash again? Is it weird now?"

Yuri rolled his eyes. "Sure, I'd fuck Ash again if you two don't give a fuck. Weird or not, what we do with our lives has nothing to do with anybody else."

"Exactly." Lance's face seemed to brighten up, adding a depth of color he didn't usually have in his pigmentless skin. Oddly enough, Yuri wasn't sure he had ever seen Lance so happy in his life.

"Stop. You have to promise," Yuri said. "I'm not part of the deal. Ash has to love you for you. Besides, you're forgetting something important. Just because this little setup would work for *you* doesn't mean it'd work for *Ash*."

Lance's gaze drifted to the ground. Yuri had cleaned up the blood, so it didn't look horrible now, but they needed to throw out the clutter. "All right, Yuri. Fine. So, are you going to tell me what really happened? How did your shoulder get fucked-up?"

A knock at the door interrupted their conversation. Lance sighed and answered it. It was Cedar.

"I told you we should have come here first," she said. She looked over her shoulder at Gale, who popped his head into the doorway as well. "After we lost Yuri's scent and everybody scattered, I figured he'd be here." She folded her arms. "It's time for retribution, tiger."

"What the hell happened?" Gale said, taking in the state of the twins and the cabin.

Lance looked back at Yuri. "What's Cedar talking about? What did you do?"

Yuri shrugged. "Ruined romance?"

CHAPTER 18

LANCE HAD CHOCOLATE ALL over his face and fingers. It all tasted good, though, and his cuts were scabbed over and healing, so he didn't care much. He never complained when it came to Cedar and food. No one did. The polar bear knew food. However, it sucked having to do all this work. He was helping to replace the chocolates that Yuri had ruined yesterday. At least making the chocolates was better than cleaning up the kitchen. Cedar had insisted they clean it top to bottom, beyond the mess Yuri had made, before getting started.

Thankfully, Cedar waited until morning so they could get some sleep last night. And it wasn't just Lance and Yuri doing all this work. Most of the shifters currently staying in Eurio were here helping. Lance had a sneaking suspicion that Cedar planned all of this out just so Yuri would be a part of everything, not really as a punishment at all.

"Are you going to tell us what happened to your face yet?" Mateo asked as he worked alongside Lance.

"You know what happened," Lance said.

"Yeah, I just want to know why."

Lance glanced over at his brother, who was working on the other side of the prep table. They had beat each other up pretty good last night, but the marks were beginning to fade already, thanks to their tiger-shifter healing. Yuri paid Lance no mind, content to focus on what he was doing. He was making some very… interesting chocolates, like abstract crystal shards or pieces of flat coral. He wanted to see what would happen if he didn't use the heart-shaped molds, so he was drizzling hot liquid chocolate over wax paper. It was mostly a disaster, but some of the shapes turned out cool. Control-freak Cedar hadn't made any comments on it—which was probably just as well.

Lance wondered what Ash was up to.

He hadn't had a chance to call with all the chaos going on. Not even in the morning. Cedar woke them

VALENTINE'S DAY TIGERS

up bright and early and didn't give them a chance to do anything for themselves.

Besides, he was doubting himself.

He realized he was being crazy about this whole thing. He tried to give Ash everything last night. He laid it all out on the table, and all of it was true. Maybe the craziest thing of all was how Ash seemed to accept him anyway. They said they'd wait for him at a hotel they hadn't planned on staying in so long. Lance could fix that and give Ash a home. Eurio was more open-minded at this point. They probably wouldn't care too much if he brought a human here in need of refuge. They had Austin, and it was *Ash* he was talking about. Everyone would fall in love with them.

"Why are you still here?" Yuri said as he let another strange piece of chocolate dry on some wax paper. "Cedar didn't make you come. She didn't have anything to use as leverage against you."

Lance ignored him and worked on mixing one of the raspberry fillings. Yuri asked a stupid question. Of course Lance was going to come here with him. It was like he said: they were a package deal. They did everything together. Mostly.

"Go to Ash already. That's what you want, right?" Yuri said. He pointed a chocolate-covered spoon at

Lance, accusing. "If you're that serious about them, maybe consider telling them you're a tiger too."

Lance gritted his teeth because there were eyes. Yuri wasn't being quiet, and everybody else, Mateo at the very least, was well within listening range.

Lance let go of his spoon and signed for Yuri to knock it off unless he wanted to take this conversation private, but Gale saw it too. It was hard to have a private conversation out in the open when ASL was a bit of a common thing in Eurio. That was what happened with Alphas like Gale and Weston and even Weston's mate, Cary. They always tried to support him and Yuri in whatever way they could.

Yuri didn't bother signing back. "Well?"

"It's probably too soon for that," Lance muttered. If Yuri was going to talk, he was going to talk and there was nothing Lance could do about it—unless he went over there and physically shut his brother's trap.

"What are you talking about?" Mateo asked like Lance knew he would. "Who's Ash?" Austin leaned forward to look past Mateo, just as curious.

"Lance's lover," Yuri said nonchalantly. "Oh, his 'secret lover.'"

Lance gritted his teeth harder. His jaw clenched to an almost painful degree.

VALENTINE'S DAY TIGERS

"Lance has a lover?" Mateo said loudly, drawing way more eyes and ears then Lance would've liked. Heat crawled up his neck, and he fidgeted with the collar of his shirt.

"Girlfriend? Boyfriend?" Mateo continued.

"Ash is non-binary," Lance said.

Mateo stared at him for a moment in disbelief. His eyes even flickered yellow and he bared his teeth. "You have a lover? How did I not know this?"

Lance cleared his throat. "It was kind of something I was keeping under wraps." He shot his brother a death glare. Yuri met that with a broad smirk.

"Why?"

"Do tell," Cedar said, probably the last shifter here who had any business demanding these kinds of answers from Lance. She had only been here a couple months.

"I think we'd all like to hear the story, Lance," Weston joined in.

Lance felt like he was suffocating. "It doesn't matter," he insisted. He tried to find that detachment he used to deal with things, but it wasn't coming. He was flustered.

"Human or shifter?" Gale asked.

"Human," Lance said. He was under verbal fire. He

166

didn't know why he was answering these questions. In the past, he wouldn't have said a word. It was because of that breakthrough last night. It was because of what happened with Ash. Ash still wanted him.

"It doesn't matter if they're shifter or human. Look at Mateo and Austin," Lance added.

"It does matter," Gale said. "Bring them here. I'd like to talk to them."

Lance would've refused that just a couple days ago, but he wanted to bring Ash here. He thought Ash might like it. Minus the shifter part. He had no idea how they would deal with that, or how soon that little piece of information should be revealed. Would the tiger revelation be the thing to make Ash leave him after all this?

Hell, the room was getting really hot. Lance dealt with plenty of anxiety, but he was usually able to keep it under the surface. Others probably didn't realize it, and that was how he liked it. He didn't like drawing attention to himself, but he was currently falling apart at the seams.

"This is stupid, right?" he said. "I'm not going to bring Ash here."

Lance stared at the raspberry concoction he had mixed more than enough. When no one said anything,

VALENTINE'S DAY TIGERS

he forced himself to look around him. All eyes were on him. Some were new. Many of them were old and familiar. It was always Lance and Yuri, but they had spent years here, and a handful of the shifters who were permanent residents had come to mean something to them, even beyond Mateo, who was brought into their innermost circle.

This was Lance's family. If he was serious about Ash, he supposed he did have to bring them here. He'd also have to reveal his tiger. It was easier to get everything out in the open sooner rather than later after last night, right? He'd have more anxiety if he prolonged it.

"Bring them to the Valentine's Day dance," Cedar said. "You don't have to bring them any sooner if you're worried, Lance. That's a perfect date opportunity, and then we'll all get to meet them without making a big deal out of it. Or you can bring Ash earlier. Whatever you're comfortable with."

Lance returned to his usual quiet when he had nothing snarky to say in return. He glanced at Yuri, who was focused once again on his chocolate creations. Monstrosities, more like.

Lance wondered why Cedar was determined to be so motherly to him, to everyone. He wondered why everyone here put up with him and Yuri and their antics, their almost innate need to be difficult in some way shape or form.

"Sappy," Lance said on impulse, drawing on that need for a front. "The Valentine's Day dance is sappy as hell."

"It's romantic," Cedar said. "Just think about it."

Lance rolled his eyes. He brought the head of the spoon he was holding to his lips and tasted the raspberry filling. Goddammit, it tasted good.

Mateo kept trying to catch his eye, but Lance wouldn't look. He was done with this. He was done with the vulnerability he had just displayed. He needed to rein it back in or else he'd fall to pieces right then and there.

But he did like Cedar's idea. Ash liked to dance. Maybe they'd like to be his Valentine, too.

CHAPTER 19

ASH TOOK ANOTHER SIP of their drink. They never drank alcohol before a show, so it was warm honey-lemon water to get the voice ready to go. They usually got lost in their head, reciting the music they'd be playing for the upcoming session. This evening, however, Ash was thinking about Lance. It wasn't an unusual thing these days. They had started thinking about him more and more as they got to know him. And after last night, it was kind of inevitable that Lance would take up so much space in Ash's musical mind. Ash thought they could probably write a hundred songs for Lance easy.

Last night, Lance was pretty upset, though. Ash

had never seen him cry. That icy wall he erected to protect himself melted down to the rawest layer, and he kept apologizing like he didn't feel validated. The fact that he didn't like sex seemed to bother him way more than it did Ash. Ash didn't really understand why, but it was obviously a sensitive topic for Lance. Ash could understand that part. Ash's body was female in every way. While they didn't hate that fact, they weren't a woman. They were just Ash. It felt wrong to be referred to as "she" or "her," though it was people's natural assumption.

Who was this "she" they were talking about?

Maybe that was part of what Ash liked about Lance and even his brother, Yuri, right away. Ash gave their pronouns and the brothers used them without asking questions. It was a nice change.

Ash wasn't asexual, but that didn't matter. Ash wasn't going to discard Lance because of that. They didn't love him any less. And they wouldn't let him run away after confessing something so personal about himself. He was afraid to tell Ash the truth, but he did anyway because he wanted to keep them. Because he loved them.

No, Ash wasn't going to let him go so easily. They had exchanged phone numbers. That meant Lance

VALENTINE'S DAY TIGERS

wasn't *planning* on running away either. Thank the universe.

Ash thought about calling almost a hundred times today, but they restrained themself. For some reason, Ash felt like Lance needed to call them first. But there was a time limit. If Lance didn't call by tomorrow, Ash would give in and call first.

"You're quiet," Frank said as he passed another hot mug of honey-lemon water over to Ash. "Writing a new song?"

"No," Ash said.

"That's unusual for you."

"Could you live without sex, Frank? In an intimate relationship."

The bar owner gave Ash a funny look; he simultaneously raised his wiry eyebrows and scowled. "Is it 'intimate' if there's no sex?"

"Yes."

"Well, we might have to agree to disagree on that. I don't know how intimate a relationship can be without sex if we're talking life partners. For a child-parent relationship, then definitely yes, without sex."

Ash stuck out their tongue. "Thanks for that. It was unnecessary."

"Hey, you're the one asking weird questions."

"I'm talking about life partners." Ash frowned. "Why is it weird?"

"Because what you're talking about is just friendship."

"But it's romantic," Ash insisted.

"Romance and sex go hand in hand."

"Not always."

Frank shook his head. "I'm having a hard time wrapping my brain around whatever you're trying to tell me, Ash. Romance is handing your girl a rose, kissing her silent, and taking her to bed."

Ash used their pointer finger to trace around the rim of their mug and watched the still liquid; it burned amber in the dim light. Ash loved being close to Lance in whatever way he'd have them. They were flattered he loved them enough to do what he did last night, but not if it was at his expense. It didn't matter how much Ash enjoyed it if Lance had hated it.

Had he *hated* it?

"What if your girl's not in the mood?" Ash asked. "Do you still love her?"

"Yeah," Frank shrugged, "but my girl likes sex, and those occasions are rare."

"What if there was an accident, involving bad paralysis or something, and sex was out of the question?

VALENTINE'S DAY TIGERS

Would you still love her, or would you leave her?"

Frank frowned. "I don't know, kid. Yes, I'd still love her. But sex... I can't imagine living without it. I take it you found someone you like, but they're not into whatever you're into."

"Something like that."

"I won't pretend to understand," at least he tried more than most, "but if you feel the same way, neither of you interested in sex, then I guess it's no problem, and you can call the relationship whatever you want. Romantic, platonic, whatever."

Ash tapped the mug. That was the thing, though. They liked Lance. They loved him, everything about him, and they were undeniably *sexually* attracted to him.

"What if I'm attracted to him, but he isn't attracted to me? He takes me on the most romantic dates. He's sweet. He gets me. He loves me, and I love him."

"No idea. Sounds rough."

Frank did have some points that Ash could agree with at least: Ash's sexual attraction and Lance's lack of it. Anything was easier in a relationship if two people felt the same way and had the same dreams and beliefs or something, right? Ash hadn't thought about that before. They had never been in this situation before.

Ash's phone rang. They retrieved it from their pocket and answered after seeing the name. "Lance."

"Hey, Ash. I'm sorry for not calling sooner."

Ash smiled as they dipped their finger into the honey-lemon water. Just hearing his voice soothed and excited them at the same time. The rich tone of his voice, remembering how beautiful it sounded when he sang, got them going.

"It's okay. It's good to hear your voice, though," Ash said and hesitated a moment before asking, "How's your brother?"

"He's fine."

"Good. I'm glad."

"Ash, do you think… do you think you'd like to see my home?"

Ash's heart leaped. "Definitely. I bet it's beautiful. I haven't been to any of the really small towns in Alaska."

"Yeah, it's pretty nice, I guess. I'll pick you up?"

"Aren't I out of your way?"

"Doesn't matter." He paused. "I'm already here, at your hotel. I couldn't wait to see you again, and I'd like to spend some time with you, alone, on the drive there, before the crazy people in my life demand to meet you."

VALENTINE'S DAY TIGERS

This was huge. It was as if Ash running off with Yuri a couple nights ago had cracked Lance right open. The secrets surrounding him were unraveling.

"Okay. Sounds perfect," Ash said.

"Thank goodness." Lance breathed a sigh of relief. "See you soon?"

"I'm at Tipsy, but I'll drive over right now. Wait for me."

"Always."

Ash hung up and pushed their unfinished drink away. "Sorry, Frank. I won't be playing tonight."

"Where are you going?"

"I don't know, but it might be home. It might be the place I've been searching for all this time."

"What? Well, at least come back from time to time if you're sticking around here, yeah?"

Ash jumped off the stool and ran out the bar door, barely tugging on their coat before getting blasted by frigid winds.

They couldn't stop grinning.

CHAPTER 20

When the last note rang out from their ukulele, Ash opened their eyes. They finally did it. They played their song for Lance. Instead of using satellite radio to get music (this SUV was fancy), Ash had serenaded him since leaving Fairbanks.

"Is that song about us?" Lance gripped the steering wheel tighter. "It better be about us."

Ash laughed. "Yes. I wrote that one for you. When I realized I love you."

Lance flicked a glance at them before returning his eyes to the road. "It's perfect."

He turned onto a small street that was hidden from the main road. It was dusted with snow, but it had

VALENTINE'S DAY TIGERS

been traveled. Still, the ride turned a bit bumpy. They passed by scattered cabins and many trees, mainly black and white spruces.

"This is Eurio," Lance said.

Ash commented, "It's so spread out."

"We like our space."

The cabins they passed all seemed to be around the same size. Ash couldn't get too good of a look at them since it was dark, but the headlights flashed ahead and cast a beam of light on another building. This one was much larger. It was either a mansion or it was something else. It didn't look fancy enough to be a mansion, and Lance pulled them into a very small covered parking lot that housed silver SUVs identical to the one Lance was driving. Maybe this was a community building, a hunting lodge or something.

When Lance killed the engine, he kept his hands on the steering wheel and didn't move. Ash didn't say anything at first. They looked at the cuts marring his face. They had asked about them as soon as they had gotten into the SUV with Lance. He answered with a vague, "I got in a fight." Ash decided not to push, but their eyes kept drifting to the claw marks on his cheek. They looked like claw marks. They also looked ridiculously deep for how much they had to have healed since last night—if that made any sense.

Ash reached over and rested their hand on top of Lance's. "Why are you so nervous?"

"I… We're a bit different in Eurio."

"I've been all over North America. I've seen many different people."

"Yeah, but probably not people like this."

"Are you afraid I won't like your family?"

"I guess."

Ash gently pried his hands off the steering wheel. "I go with the flow, and I like everybody just fine."

"I guess you'd have to, hanging out at a bar every night." Lance offered a small smile.

Ash grinned. "Everybody has an interesting story to tell. I used to let the universe guide me around and take me all over. I met a lot of people, but no one ever stuck. It was just me and my ukulele. Then the universe led me to you, and now I think I want you to guide me for a while."

"What are you talking about?" Lance laughed.

"I'm saying that life is a crazy journey, but it led me to you. I want you."

Lance reclaimed his hands and brushed away a couple of stray curly hairs that had found their way in front of Ash's eyes. "Ash, have I ever told you you're

VALENTINE'S DAY TIGERS

beautiful?"

Ash had been told they were beautiful before, but mostly by drunk guys at bars who had a certain fetish. Ash didn't know their parents, but whatever genes they had gave them a bit of a unique look, they supposed. Those "compliments" may have been genuine, and they may not have been, but Lance's words certainly were. No one looked at Ash the way he did. It wasn't heat— though it translated as such in Ash's body. It was something else.

It was love.

Ash blew out a breath of air, trying to cool the hot flash. "You haven't."

"Well, I should have. I'll get better at this."

Ash already thought he was quite good. They had never met anyone more loving than him. "I like you being open like this." Ash pressed their thumb against Lance's lips. "Are kisses off limits? Do you like them or dislike them?"

Lance replied by stealing Ash's hand away so he could lean forward and kiss them. It was the same brush on lips, soft sucking, alternating between Ash's top and bottom lip. When Lance pulled away, he said, "I like some kisses. I'm not a huge fan of tongue, though."

"Sweet kisses, then," Ash said. They pulled him in for another kiss, mirroring what Lance had just done.

There was no denying that Ash loved any kind of kiss they could get from Lance. Knowing that he wasn't completely against them was nice. Some of that heat Ash felt last night returned, and they reflexively squeezed their thighs. They tried to tone down their need, but it wasn't working. Ash moved back before the feelings got too intense. Maybe this would be a little bit of a challenge after all.

Lance studied Ash in silence for a moment. "We call this place the Lodge. It's, uh, where I'll introduce you to everyone. Ready to get out?"

"Yep."

Ash, zipped up their coat, put on their gloves, grabbed their ukulele, and exited the SUV. Ash was about to join Lance on the other side since he was closer to the front door of the Lodge, but movement caught their eye. It came from the black and white spruces. Ash squinted to see past the darkness. It must have helped because they caught sight of a white blur that almost blended in with the snow, until it came closer and closer. It was furry and round and cute and—a polar bear cub.

"Do you see that?" Ash pointed.

VALENTINE'S DAY TIGERS

Lance came around to join them on their side of the SUV and said, "Oh shit."

The polar bear cub seemed to just notice them as it held out its paws to the snow, sliding to a stop just feet from them. It stared at Lance and then at Ash.

"Get out of here," Lance said sternly.

"You really think a little polar bear is going to listen to what you have to say?" Ash asked. "Oh my god, Lance. A baby *polar* bear. Do polar bears live in Alaska?" Ash pulled out their phone, determined to take a picture. This was Instagram worthy. Everyone who followed Ash on social media was going to eat this up. Ash didn't know their followers personally, but they had met some of them in their travels. If Ash had had a family, they were it. No matter how far removed, they were just a screen tap away.

Ash was about to snap that photo, but Lance grabbed their wrist and ruined the shot.

"Hey," Ash said, "I can take a quick photo before we get the hell out of here. I'm sure its mama isn't far behind."

"Sorry, Ash, but that's not it. Please, no pictures." Lance's throat bobbed as he swallowed.

Ash had no idea what that was about, but Lance seemed stressed about it, so they put their phone in their pocket just as a big brown and gray wolf darted out of the trees. It let out a growling bark, and its ears pointed forward. Its yellow eyes were trained on the cub as it salivated.

"What the hell?" Ash stepped forward, getting ready to save the polar bear cub if the wolf was hunting it. But then the wolf's gaze flickered up to Ash and Lance, and it skidded to a stop beside the polar bear cub. The cub leaned into the wolf like they were old friends. It even wrapped a paw around the wolf's foreleg. The wolf rested its chin atop the cub's head. It was the most precious thing Ash had ever seen in their life. What the hell was going on?

"Get the fuck out of here, you two," Lance gritted out.

"Do you know them?" Ash asked. Lance was upset, but he didn't seem scared of these wild animals. Not in the slightest. He was talking to them as if they were his pets or something. As if they understood his words, the polar bear cub and wolf backed away. And then there was a tiger. A goddamn orange Siberian tiger came bounding out of the trees. Compared to this muscular killing machine, the wolf was as small as a puppy—and the wolf was huge.

"Do you have a private zoo out here?" Ash asked.

VALENTINE'S DAY TIGERS

Lance was right about one thing: they had never seen anything like this in their life, and they weren't sure how they should be reacting right now. This tiger was *big*, though. Very. Big.

Ash took a step back as the tiger loped toward them, tail flicking back and forth like a snake about to bite.

CHAPTER 21

"**L**ANCE," ASH SAID, GRABBING his coat sleeve and yanking. "Let's get inside, yeah?"

"I'm so sorry." Lance put his hand on top of Ash's as if to reassure them, but he wouldn't budge. It was like his feet were stuck in dried concrete. It didn't matter how hard Ash yanked. "You can go inside the Lodge if you want. I'll meet you there in a minute."

"What are you talking about? I'm not leaving you out here alone."

Then Ash saw the tiger's eyes. They were like a sunburst.

Fire reflected in those eyes.

"This tiger looks familiar," Ash said. They realized

VALENTINE'S DAY TIGERS

that sounded insane, but they weren't exactly known to be the most "normal" person in the world.

"Familiar?" Lance frowned. "You recognize him like this?" He quickly shook his head before Ash could ask him to explain what he meant. "Never mind. Yep, let's go inside." He turned Ash around with ease, despite them digging in their heels, and called over his shoulder, "Did you hear? We're going inside. Now is *not* the time for this."

A roar sounded, loud and deafening. Ash covered their ears with their hands. Sounds like gunfire followed, or maybe it was large tree branches snapping under the weight of snow.

"Why wait?" a deep and familiar voice said. "It would be easier to get this all out of the way first thing, wouldn't it? I'm doing you a favor."

Ash wriggled their way out of Lance's hold to look back at where the tiger was just standing. Now there was a naked tattooed man. It was Yuri.

"Hi again," he said. His eyes flashed the same fire-orange as the tiger's, and he had a predatory grin on his lips.

Ash stared at his sharp canines as they peeked out from his beard. They hesitated a moment before saying back, "Hi." They blinked a few times, trying to make

186

sense of what had just happened. The polar bear cub and wolf hadn't left and seemed intent on watching this entire exchange. Both of their heads were cocked.

"What the fuck are you doing?!" Lance exclaimed.

"Ash has a right to know. Right, Ash?" Yuri said.

"So, wait a minute. You're a tiger?" Ash rubbed their temples. They were feeling lightheaded and stumbled when they took a step backward. Lance caught them.

"Yes, I'm a tiger," Yuri said. "Well, technically, I'm a tiger *shifter*." He folded his strong arms as goosebumps raised his skin. He was naked in the freezing cold. *Naked.* Apparently, that was a very normal thing for him, but he still had goosebumps.

"Are you cold?" was the only thing Ash could think to say.

Yuri laughed. "That's what you're focused on?"

Ash pinched their arm. "Well, I don't seem to be dreaming."

"Oh my god," Lance lamented. "Why, Yuri? I think Ash is in shock."

"I didn't plan this out, okay? I was playing with Ike, Mateo joined us, and then we ran into you guys. Seemed like the perfect opportunity. Ash can handle it."

VALENTINE'S DAY TIGERS

Ash didn't know if they were in shock or if they were going nuts. They knew they should have been questioning this more. Maybe running and screaming or hijacking an SUV and hightailing it out of there. But Lance was still with them, holding them. Apparently, that was all the reassurance they needed.

Yes, a minute ago there was a tiger standing where Yuri now stood, the same Yuri Ash had recklessly run off with. Also, he had similar cuts to Lance all over his body. So, the fight Lance had talked about was between the two of them. As tigers... That explained the claw marks.

Ash stared. They weren't thinking about it at first, but it was hard not to admire Yuri's body when it was on full display like this. And it was hard not to remember that night. Ash couldn't stop the flush of heat that went through their body. Sex with Yuri had been good. Ash had been wild. They had fed off Yuri's energy. It was very different from sex with Lance.

The brothers didn't look much alike at a glance. They didn't act much alike either. What had they been fighting about to get cut up like that? Was it about Ash? Lance said he wasn't mad, but what if...

Ash felt guilty. They forced their eyes away from Yuri and turned to Lance. "Are you a tiger 'shifter' too?"

"Yes. I didn't want you to find out like this. Are you okay? You look pale." He touched Ash's cheek. His touch felt the same, warm and comforting. Ash didn't flinch away and took his hand. They would go along with this. That was how they lived. They went with the flow, and this was Lance. The same Lance they had come here for. The same Lance they were taking a chance on.

"Show me," Ash whispered.

Lance nodded after searching Ash's eyes for a moment longer. Ash didn't know what he was looking for, but they held his gaze. Then he stripped off his coat and his clothes and immediately dropped down to the snow. That same loud cracking noise filled the air as his skin rippled. His body morphed and Ash took a step back because he just kept getting bigger. Where a man was, a tiger began to emerge. The shape came first, then fur sprouted all over his body. He grew a long and powerful tail, big teeth, and sharp claws. He looked much like his brother in this form, but the base color of his fur was white, and his eyes maintained that ice blue.

He was huge. Ash almost took another step back, but they stood their ground. Lance was right next to them. They could reach out and touch his fur. It somehow made all of that muscle look soft and inviting.

VALENTINE'S DAY TIGERS

Lance didn't move, but he watched and his tail twitched back and forth. Ash reached out for him, afraid, yes, but they needed to know if he felt like the Lance they knew. Ash touched his big head, between his rounded ears. Aside from the fur, the warmth they felt was the same.

Lance moved forward to rub his body against Ash. He was careful about how much strength he put behind it, but Ash almost fell over anyway. They would have if Lance hadn't been there to catch them. Ash stayed slumped over his back, unable to get back up on their own feet. They could hardly feel their feet. This was the craziest and coolest moment of Ash's life.

"I can't believe this is real. This is real," they said as they grabbed fistfuls of Lance's fur and mashed their cheek against his powerful body. They were hugging a potentially dangerous tiger like he was one of those life-size stuffed animals. Lance nudged Ash's hips with his head, and Ash found their feet.

Yuri folded his arms and grinned. The polar bear cub and wolf were no longer animals either. Ash missed their change, but they saw a little boy and another muscular, tattooed man in their place. Though they had changed so much, there were aspects of them that stayed the same. Their eyes, the way they carried themselves, it was all the same.

"Holy fuck," Ash said. "This is what you meant when you said Eurio is different. And you are right. I have never seen anything like this in my life."

"That's one way to introduce everyone," a deep voice sounded from behind. Ash got up and turned around, but they kept one hand in Lance's fur. A big man and woman, and several others, came from around the corner. They must have come from the front of the Lodge. The man didn't look pleased. He wore a slight scowl.

"Why don't you come inside with everyone, Ash," the man said. "We can talk where it's warm."

"Good idea, Gale," Yuri said. "I'm freezing my ass off."

Lance stepped forward, toward the newcomers, as if he intended to lead the way. Since Ash continued clinging to his fur and stumbled along beside him, it was true enough. It seemed Ash was going into the Lodge with a bunch of people who could turn into animals. Ash was surprisingly okay with that, and it was all because of Lance.

CHAPTER 22

ASH SAT BESIDE LANCE as Cedar grilled them on all sorts of things. She had all kinds of questions: where was Ash from, what was their history, what were they going to do with this new-found shifter knowledge? Lance wanted to tell Cedar to stop, but Ash was eager to engage.

"I never knew my parents. I grew up in the foster care system," Ash said. "I don't have a family unless you call the people who follow me on social media family. I kind of do. The internet can offer an amazing support group among all the chaos."

"Did you take a picture?" Cedar asked, gesturing to Ash's cell phone.

"No. Lance stopped me. And I won't try to take any more. I'll break my phone if it'll make you feel better." Ash held out their hand and almost turned it over to drop their phone on the ground. They even had their foot raised, boot ready to smash it. Lance grabbed their hand, closing Ash's fingers around their phone before they could follow through.

"That is not necessary," Lance said quickly. He was moved that Ash would go to such lengths, though. Their heart rate was steady, so it wouldn't have been done out of fear.

"Whatever it takes," Ash said. "I want to stay a while. Please, let me stay." Ash studied Lance, and Lance wondered if it was because they were trying to see the tiger in the human part of him. "But it's so weird. I always just kind of babied animals, you know? I wonder what they really have going through their heads. Hope I never offended any shifters."

Weston chuckled. "You are a strange one, Ash."

Austin pushed his glasses up his nose and said, "You're taking this remarkably well."

Ash snuggled closer to Lance and took his hand. He squeezed in response. "It's because it feels like nothing's really changed. This is still Lance, the same guy I met a few months ago and... fell in love with."

VALENTINE'S DAY TIGERS

"Months ago," Gale echoed. He studied Lance with a hard gaze. "Months ago?" he repeated.

"I'm good at hiding things?" Lance offered.

"No shit," Mateo said.

"Do you promise to keep us a secret, Ash?" Cedar asked.

"Cross my heart and hope to die."

Cedar nodded. "All right."

"I always have my head in the clouds. That's what people say anyway, so even if I did say something, I promise you have nothing to fear from me. No one's going to believe my fairytales."

"You don't have to keep trying to sell your sincerity," Lance said. "Cedar already knows. She's been making this go on longer than necessary because she's paranoid."

"I'm not paranoid," Cedar defended. "You are. I'm just doing my job."

"She knows I'm sincere?" Ash asked.

"Yes," Cedar replied. "Shifters are good judges of character. We're also pretty good at picking out lies."

"Okay, because if you're not convinced," Ash held out their hands, wrists up, "I'll even be a prisoner. Just don't send me back out into the wild. I want to stay."

"Where did you find this person?" Weston asked.

"Fairbanks," Lance and Ash replied in unison.

Ash continued, "But I've traveled a lot, and I've seen a lot of things, though never anything like this."

Ash wasn't the kind of person Lance would describe as excitable. It wasn't that they didn't get excited, but they had a levelness about everything they did. They took things in stride, but they were positively energized at the moment. Lights danced in their green eyes.

"No prisoners," Gale said. "You are good to go, Ash. We believe what you've said, and you're welcome to stay here in Eurio. The Lenkovs would be happy to have you, I'm sure."

"Since I passed interrogation, does that mean I get to ask a few questions?" Ash asked.

"Not yet. Sorry. Some things are better left said on a need-to-know basis. Plus, it's getting late."

Ash didn't push, and Weston dismissed everyone.

Yuri hadn't said a word the whole time they were in the Lodge. There were spare clothes kept inside, so he wasn't forced to stay in his tiger form or sit naked in his human form. He was cozied up in his coat once he got it on. Then he had started dozing off. At Weston's dismissal, he was suddenly awake and the first one to leave.

VALENTINE'S DAY TIGERS

Lance watched him go, but he didn't chase after him. He took Ash's hand and walked out with them in their own time. But, before they could escape, Mateo grabbed Lance's arm.

"'Have you met me?'" he mocked. "'I've never been in love.' Bullshit."

Lance tore away from him. "It's complicated. I didn't mean to hide it. It's just… it's complicated."

Ash smiled. "I'm glad I finally got to meet one of Lance's closest friends."

"Me too," Mateo said.

Austin came forward and caught Mateo's hand. "Welcome to the crazy life of shifters, Ash. I hope you stick around. It would be nice to add another human to this family." Austin turned to Lance, but he couldn't quite meet his gaze. "I'm sorry for misjudging you."

"I think you've judged me just fine," Lance remarked. It wasn't like he had changed any now that Ash was in the picture. He was still him.

"I plan on sticking around," Ash said. Then they grabbed Lance's waist and stood on their tiptoes. Lance leaned down for a quick kiss like Ash so obviously wanted. He wasn't lying about enjoying some kisses, so he was just as eager. These kisses were the absolute best because they were shared with Ash, though. Ash cut the kiss short, taking to heart what he had said in the SUV. He wasn't sure how to feel about that. Ash was being careful with him now.

"Did you ask Ash to the dance?" Austin said.

"Yeah, did you?" Mateo joined. "Austin brings it up every day."

"Hey, one of us has to bring the romance into this relationship."

"Yep."

"There's going to be a dance?" Ash asked.

"Yeah, for Valentine's," Lance said. "And I was going to ask. Just hadn't found the right time, but whatever. Guess I'm asking now. Will you be my date to Eurio's Valentine's Day dance, Ash?"

"I will. You know I love dancing."

"Yeah, I do. And you're good at it."

"You're not half bad yourself."

"See you both at the dance, then," Austin said and turned to his mate. "Take me home, handsome."

Mateo grinned, and then he swept Austin off his feet and into his arms. Austin let out a short shriek. "Warn me before you do that!"

"You told me to take you home." Mateo rubbed his nose against his mate's, playfully disheveling his green-rimmed glasses. Austin smiled softly.

"Let's go, Ash," Lance said. "These two are gross."

"You're not any better," Mateo said.

Lance shook his head and gave Mateo a small shove. Mateo looked back at him and grinned, eyes flashing yellow, and then he went on his way with his mate securely in his arms.

By the time Lance and Ash were back on course, Yuri was way ahead of them. He was nothing but a dot in the dark. Lance was sure Ash couldn't see him since they were limited by their human sight, but they were content to walk alongside Lance, trusting him to lead the way. Not even Lance could pick out Yuri's features this far away, but he knew how his brother walked; his long, confident gait was seared into Lance's mind.

In some ways, Lance knew Yuri like the back of his hand. In other ways, he was a mystery.

Lance wondered what was going through Yuri's head right now.

Yuri clicked the next link for another one of those video montages of people doing stupid things and getting themselves hurt. He found it entertaining, but not after watching several of them. Not to mention the internet was basically slow as hell out here, compared to Fairbanks anyway. However, paying attention to Lance and Ash was worse.

Since Lance and Yuri had totaled their couch, Gale had pulled out an old bean bag from the Lodge storage for them. Lance and Ash were sitting on it, cuddling and being gross. Yuri never complained about Austin and Mateo out loud like Lance did, but he wasn't a fan of all this mushy stuff.

"Do you remember how we met?" Ash asked.

"Definitely," Lance said. "You ran into me when you got your drink after a show and spilled it all over my shirt."

"Yeah, that was funny. I'm glad I did. If I hadn't, we probably never would've talked."

"Yeah, me too."

Ash sat snugly on Lance's lap, and they stared into each other's eyes as they reminisced about all the little things they had done together, all these things Yuri had no idea Lance was doing in Fairbanks. Lance never left when Yuri was bad off, but he had left plenty when Yuri was doing well enough to hang around with Mateo or cause trouble elsewhere in Eurio. Yuri could have gone with Lance. It wasn't like Lance tried to hide it, but

VALENTINE'S DAY TIGERS

Fairbanks wasn't as fun for him when PWD was a thing in his life. And not just that. He got tired of making Lance deal with his shit whenever he'd have a seizure out there. Lance would have to get him back to Eurio on his own somehow because it always came in waves.

"Every time I went to Fairbanks, I hoped I'd see you there," Lance said.

"And I started showing up at the library and the bar, just waiting for you to get there," Ash replied.

God, it was a sappy love story if Yuri ever heard one. But he was happy for his brother. For so long he had chained Lance down, and it seemed Ash had finally set him free.

The world was cruel.

Yuri clicked out of the videos he was watching and closed the web browser. Then he turned off the computer and pressed his hand to his aching head. He had been dealing with a dull headache for the majority of the day. He was thinking about turning in for the night. It was probably for the best. He could leave Ash and Lance to it.

When he looked back at his brother and the human he'd fallen in love with, still cuddling, he said, "How long can two people stare into each other's eyes?"

That got the two of them to tear their gaze away

from each other. Yuri called that a win. At least they'd hear him. "I'm going to bed. Have fun, kids, but not too much or I'll get jealous that you left me with the boring part."

"Sorry, Yuri," Lance said quickly.

Yuri shrugged. He didn't know why his brother was apologizing. Yuri was just teasing.

"You've been quiet. You don't usually stare at videos for that long."

Yuri decided to tell the truth. "I have a headache."

Apparently, "headache" was a trigger because Lance frowned so deep that Yuri was afraid his face would melt off.

"It's a headache caused by boredom," Yuri amended, hoping it'd get his easily agitated brother to chill out. He was so high-strung.

"We can do something that includes all of us," Ash said. "Truth or dare. Unless your headache is too bad, Yuri."

Truth or dare? Yuri grinned. "I'm in."

"Okay, Yuri," Ash said. "Truth or dare."

"Dare of course."

"Mix together all of the beverages in the house and drink down a full glass of it."

"That's easy." And nasty. Yuri got up and headed

VALENTINE'S DAY TIGERS

to the kitchen. Ash followed with Lance on their heels. They had to make sure that he followed through and didn't cheat. Besides, watching a dare get executed was most of the fun.

Yuri opened the fridge and took a look at what was inside. Then he pulled out milk, some vegetable concoction that was supposed to be good for you (if you were a human maybe), a green tea, and a flat soda. Gross. They had more beverages than usual, but Yuri would get it down quick.

He mixed equal portions of them into a glass; it was a lovely puke green color when it was finished. Then he plugged his nose and tipped his head back, drinking the whole thing in a few well-timed gulps. Getting it down was okay, but the aftertaste was revolting. Ash didn't specify any rules against drinking water to clear his palate after the dare, so he did that next.

"Gross," Ash said, grinning. "You did that like a champ. You didn't even gag."

"I'll get you back for it, though," Yuri said. But for now, he turned to Lance. Lance folded his arms and waited. "Truth or dare, bro?"

He did exactly what Yuri was counting on. "Truth."

"Boring. What do you want out of this little three-some?"

Lance cleared his throat when Ash raised an eyebrow at him. "It's not a threesome. I just want to find a way to make this work. I want to keep both of you. Truth or dare, Ash?"

Ash glanced at Yuri and said, "Truth."

Good. Ash caught on quick. Lance probably wouldn't break the rules of the game, so this was the perfect opportunity to get everything out in the open without any pussyfooting.

"Do you like Yuri?" Lance asked. "You know, the sex. Was it good and would you do it again? Because I don't mind."

"Rambling," Yuri muttered and folded his arms. "Two questions are past the legal limit."

"But they were pretty much the same question," Lance defended. "And since when do we follow the rules? Rules are for bending or breaking, right?"

Ash scowled. "Lance, sex doesn't break us, okay? I told you that already, and I mean it."

That was exactly what Yuri wanted to hear. There was no stutter in the steady rhythm of Ash's heartbeat.

Yuri clapped his brother on the shoulder. "And there you have it. You heard Ash, so stop worrying."

VALENTINE'S DAY TIGERS

Then Yuri turned to Ash and pointed a finger at them. "You can stay. You pass. I'll let you have my brother if that's what you both want, just don't break his heart or I'll have to wreck some shit."

"I'd never," Ash said resolutely. Yuri liked the gleam in their pretty eyes. It held fire, the same fire he ignited the night they first met. "Lance, truth or dare?"

"Dare."

A wicked grin spread across Ash's lips. "I dare you to 'shift' and eat all of this chocolate pudding I found in the fridge. With a spoon."

"When did you even snatch that?" Lance asked.

"You just want to see Lance naked again," Yuri said.

"I mean, yeah, I wouldn't mind that at all. Also, I think this will be funny and probably impossible."

"We'll see about that," Lance growled. He got to work stripping down and discarding his clothes onto the ground. Then he dashed into the living room where there was enough room for him to shift without destroying everything, as long as he stayed still. Yuri grabbed a spoon. Then he and Ash went into the living room too, after the crackling noises stopped, and squeezed past Lance's big cat body. Lance sat like a dog on command, but he had a hard time keeping his tail in place. He glanced at Yuri, and Yuri got the message. He cleared anything that might accidentally get busted. They didn't need to wreck their place again so soon.

Lance's big paws rested on the wood floor. They were *really* big, and the spoon was *so* small. Yuri had to admit Ash had a good idea after all. This was going to be amusing.

CHAPTER 23

"I'LL BE NICE AND open the lid for you, Lance," Ash said.

"No, don't," Yuri said.

"The lid wasn't part of my dare, though."

"Fine. Whatever. Do what you want."

Once the pudding cup was prepped, Yuri held out the metallic spoon to his brother. "Think you can take this?"

Lance let out a low rumble as he held up one of his big black-striped white paws and slowly extended one of his claws. It didn't work out too well. So, he resorted to curling his cat fingers into his paw, doing his best to copy the grip he'd used as a human. With that, he somehow managed to take the spoon from Yuri's hand without dropping it.

"Look at you," Yuri said, already amused.

Ash set the pudding cup down in front of Lance. Lance moved it around with his free paw as he clung desperately to the spoon with his other. He was trying to find the best angle for his foreleg so he'd actually be able to get the spoon into the cup. It was awkward, something he had clearly never tried in his tiger body. When he finally went for it, he missed the tiny pudding cup and hit the ground next to it. Lance showed his teeth and let out a low growl.

Yuri and Ash started laughing as he jabbed the spoon down and missed time and time again. When he finally did manage to get a spoonful of chocolate pudding, getting it into his mouth was almost as big of an obstacle. The spoon slipped, and chocolate got all over his white fur, but he tried again. This time, he got it into his mouth and licked off the pudding triumphantly.

Yuri laughed one of those big belly laughs. He couldn't stop, and Ash was with him. He hadn't laughed like this in a while. He couldn't breathe, so he ended up on the floor, clutching his side. Tears leaked out of his eyes when Lance went to do it all over again. He had to

VALENTINE'S DAY TIGERS

finish the cup. That was the dare. Yuri's stomach ached by the time Lance completed the dare. He quickly licked his paw and cleaned his face thoroughly before shifting back to his human form.

"Fuck." Lance shook out his hand. "I've got a shitty cramp now. You know how tightly I was holding on to that damn spoon?"

He was more worried about shaking the cramp out of his hand than getting dressed again. That was what got Ash to stop laughing. They silently took Lance in, appreciating every inch of him. The smell of their arousal hit Yuri's nose like a freight train, and his body reacted in turn. But he ignored it.

He wondered what that meant for Ash. He wondered if it was painful for them to have this strong of a physical reaction to his brother and yet have his brother decline sex. That was for the two of them to figure out, though. It had nothing to do with him.

"Your turn, Lance," Yuri said when his brother was wearing pants.

"It's bedtime," Lance said. "You look like you're about to pass out."

With all the laughing, Yuri hadn't realized how bad the throbbing in his head had gotten, but apparently it was showing on the outside. Lance knew him too well and watched him too closely.

"I'm fine," Yuri insisted.

"Bedtime."

"Killjoy. I'll take the spare room."

Lance frowned. "What?"

"Seriously, Lance?"

Ash looked back and forth between the brothers, but they stayed silent.

"We always sleep together," Lance said.

"Yeah, as a security thing left over from when we were cubs on the streets. We should grow up someday, right?"

Lance looked wounded. Truth be told, Yuri didn't fancy sleeping by himself either. Sleeping back to back, just feeling the barest hint of Lance's body heat, meant everything was okay at night. He knew the behavior was abnormal and honestly unnecessary. Lance knew it too, but they had never cared. Fitting in had never been their priority, but Lance had someone he wanted now, a potential mate, and that meant things had to change.

"We could all squeeze onto the bed together," Ash suggested.

"Not enough room," Yuri said.

"We can make it work," Lance said.

VALENTINE'S DAY TIGERS

Yuri shook his head. What was Ash trying to do? There was no way Lance would let this go if Ash didn't take Yuri's side. Yuri acquiesced. His head hurt too much to argue.

After everyone was done with the bathroom, Yuri last, Yuri walked into his and Lance's room, though he meant to go to the extra room despite what Lance and Ash had "decided." It was out of habit that he didn't. Their bed was against the wall. Ash had gone for that side, and they were already sound asleep based on how long, smooth, and calm their breathing was. Lance was cozied up next to them, the big spoon. Ash was almost smashed against the wall. It didn't look comfortable to Yuri, but clearly they didn't mind.

Yuri turned back around, ready to tiptoe out of there since Lance's back was turned to him. But Lance somehow saw him out of the corner of his eye and said with a low growl, "Come back."

"It's really not a big deal," Yuri murmured. "I'll be fine, and you'll be fine. More than fine."

Lance looked over his shoulder without moving the rest of his body. "Come back." When Yuri looked into those icy blue eyes, he saw a cub, the Lance who had always been by his side. Even when their father was alive, they had always slept together in one big cluster of bodies. It seemed to be the Lenkov way.

Yuri rolled his eyes but stepped forward. He crawled onto the bed. Somehow, he fit. The bed was bigger than he thought, or Lance was really squishing Ash, because he still had breathing room—which was the way he liked it. Even when sleeping so close together, he liked a sliver of space. He just wanted to be able to feel the heat radiating off Lance's skin, to know that he was there.

Right away, Yuri's eyelids grew heavy. This was what safety felt like. It could put him to sleep in an instant.

Lance elbowed Yuri in the back.

"What?" Yuri hissed.

"Do you like Ash?"

"Yes. You already asked me this. Stop worrying. Nothing important is going to change, all right? I'm your brother and always be." Yuri rolled over, while somehow making sure to stay in his designated space, and grabbed Lance's shoulder. He pressed his forehead into the back of Lance's neck.

"That's what I should be telling you," Lance said.

"I'm not the one obsessing over stupid things."

"If you and Ash ever do want to do anything, sex, you know, whatever, I really don't care."

VALENTINE'S DAY TIGERS

Yuri licked just below Lance's hairline. Lance jerked, but he steadied himself while silently cursing.

Wow, Yuri thought. *He really doesn't want to wake Ash up.*

"You're such an asshole," Lance whispered. "Stop trying to distract me. I could smell it, you know? Both of your arousal."

"Got it already." Yuri gave Lance's shoulder a nudge and rolled over again so his back was facing Lance. "Shut up and go to sleep."

Thankfully, Lance didn't speak another word. Yuri closed his eyes, aware of his brother's presence behind him, aware that everything was fine as long as they were together because they had each other's backs.

Everything was warm and right until the nightmares came.

CHAPTER 24

ASH STARTLED AWAKE WHEN the bed moved. It took them a moment to realize what was going on. There was a warm arm around their waist. They had never woken up like this before. Ash blinked a few times and let the weight of that warmth wash over them.

Lance.

He was fast asleep, so who was rocking the bed?

Ash stayed still, staring at the wall in front of them. They heard the door squeak open and close again with a soft click. It had to be Yuri. Ash wouldn't have worried about it. There were many reasons why he might be getting up during the night, but then they heard

VALENTINE'S DAY TIGERS

shuffling in the living room like Yuri was grabbing his coat or something.

What was he doing? It was dark outside. Ash carefully wiggled out of Lance's hold so they could look over him and to the analog clock on the headboard. The red numbers said it was three in the morning.

Ash gently took Lance's hand, rested his arm on his side, emerged from the blanket, and climbed over him—though escaping his warmth was the last thing they wanted to do. They had to check out what was going on. Something didn't seem right. Ash gave Lance's forehead a soft kiss before leaving the bed. Ash had barely touched the doorknob when they heard another door close.

In the living room, they saw Yuri's coat and boots missing. They peeked out the window but couldn't see anything in the dark. Ash grabbed their phone and quickly put on their own coat and boots to follow. They found footprints and kept their eyes low to the ground so they wouldn't lose sight of them.

Ash picked up the pace and continued following Yuri for a time, even after his tracks led into a section of extremely dense black and white spruces. Ash fished their phone out to turn on the flashlight. The trees were blocking out the light of the moon and stars above, but their phone battery was dead, so Ash was left to fumble around in the dark. They could hardly see anything at all now. They considered turning around, but they stumbled, and their sense of direction was skewed. They tried to find Yuri's tracks again, but they couldn't differentiate from disturbed snow and actual footprints. It was just too goddamn dark.

Well, they were lost.

They had no idea which way would lead them back to the Lenkovs' cabin, to Yuri, or anything else for that matter. They didn't know how far the trees would stay dense like this either.

It was time for a different approach. Ash had meant to follow Yuri quietly, but the situation had changed. Maybe he would hear them if they called his name. They were about to do it, but there was movement in the distance. Ash started moving again. It had to be Yuri.

When he didn't slow down, Ash was about to call his name. Then they lost their footing. The ground crumbled, and they were falling. They managed to twist their body around and dig their fingers into a solid piece of the crumbling edge. They let out a startled, "Whoa," and slid farther, until their palms were hanging off the edge. Their fingers were the only thing

VALENTINE'S DAY TIGERS

stopping them from falling into some deep hole. They couldn't tell how far down it went, but their feet weren't touching ground, so letting go seemed like a bad idea.

Ash wasn't the screaming type. They held still and thought for a moment, analyzing their situation. They tried to pull themself up, but it was too slippery. Any minor movements they made had them slipping again. The gloves they wore made their grip worse. Oh, and their fingers were burning and shaking. If they gave another inch, Ash would drop down.

"This is not good," Ash remarked.

And then Yuri appeared, looking down at them, eyes flickering orange. "What are you doing?" he asked.

"Hanging out."

Yuri grinned, and then he grabbed Ash's wrists. Ash felt secure, so they stopped clawing at snow and dirt and twisted their hands to grab his wrists in return. Yuri hauled them up quickly, and Ash wasn't ready. They tried to catch their feet on the ground, but it shifted. Yuri yanked their arms away from the ditch, and Ash slammed into his hard chest as the edge crumbled away, making the hole's mouth wider.

"Well, that was precarious." Yuri let Ash go and took a step back.

Ash squinted. "What's with all these holes?" They could see another not too far away.

"I don't know. I hoped they weren't real. I thought someone else would have seen them by now if they were, but they aren't near the Toran Pack's trails, so I guess there's no reason anyone would have noticed them." Yuri winced.

"Are you okay?"

"Fine."

His cheeks looked hot, or they were so cold that they turned a bright red against his naturally tan skin tone. Ash reached up and touched his cheek. He flinched, and Ash half expected him to move away, but he stayed there, allowing Ash to rest their hand on his cheek. Ash hesitated before moving to his forehead. His skin was *hot*. Fire-hot.

"You have a fever," Ash said.

"Just a little one. I'm fine."

Ash frowned and withdrew their hand. "Now I understand why you were talking about living every moment like it's your last. Conquering the fire ahead of you. Facing every obstacle and proving you'll come out on top. Lance told me about you before, but when I met you, I didn't think you were his Yuri. You were sick for a long time."

VALENTINE'S DAY TIGERS

Yuri shoved his hands into his pockets. "I didn't get that life philosophy because I was sick. I always thought like that. It just got stronger after I got sick. I was determined not to spend the rest of whatever time I had in bed."

That fit him. Ash didn't know Yuri well, just what Lance had told them and what they had learned about him that night…

Memories of what they did flooded back into Ash's mind. Ash got hot, remembering how good Yuri's body felt against theirs, how good it felt for him to be inside of them. It was rough, the opposite of how Lance handled them, but it was exactly what Ash had needed at the time.

But Lance was who they wanted.

"Why did Lance say that to you, Yuri?" Ash asked.

"Say what?"

"He asked if you liked me and said he wouldn't mind if the two of us got together."

"As shifters, we're acutely aware of sexual attraction. Even if it doesn't turn Lance on, he can smell the way your body reacts. Hell, he can smell the way my body reacts."

Ash cleared their throat. "That's… a little awkward."

Yuri showed his teeth. Ash couldn't call it a grin. "Yes. I can smell your need right now."

Ash self-consciously drew their thighs together. "But why did he say it? It's like he *wants* me to have sex with you."

"Lance is insecure about the whole sex thing. It seems like a big deal to a lot of mates, lovers, all the ones we know anyway." Yuri nodded. "He really loves you, and he wants you to be happy. That's just how Lance works."

"I told him it didn't matter, that no sex wasn't a deal-breaker."

"You sure did."

"It's… I don't know."

Yuri waited.

"I'm attracted to Lance."

"Uh-huh."

"Do you think that makes him more insecure?"

"Maybe."

"You're a good brother, aren't you?"

Yuri shrugged. "Probably not, because your scent is driving me crazy right now, and I'd really like to fuck you."

Ash laughed. "If I wasn't so in love with your brother, I'd take you up on that. Lance might not mind,

VALENTINE'S DAY TIGERS

but I do."

"See? I told him he wasn't thinking about this the right way. You should tell him that sometime." Yuri glanced up at a small clearing in the snowy branches overhead. "I like you, Ash. You're definitely going to make my brother happy. I can see it already. I can't believe it took Lance this long to make a move. You've already decided you're going to stay, haven't you?"

"Yeah, I am. As long as Lance will let me."

"He'll let you. He wants you to." Yuri looked up for a second time. There was nothing but dark sky. "Maybe it's time for me to leave Eurio."

"And leave Lance behind?" Ash asked.

"Never behind. Let him go. He's been stuck with me for years. I don't want him to feel like he has to be anymore."

Ash took both of Yuri's hands. "I can tell you right now that Lance does not feel like you're chaining him down. He loves you. You're his world."

"Not true anymore, but it doesn't matter."

Yuri froze. Footsteps crunched in the snow, and Ash squinted in the darkness to see him: Lance.

"Hey," he said.

Yuri saluted.

A grin overtook Ash's face, and they ran to Lance.

They took his hand, and Lance wrapped an arm around them, holding them even closer. It felt right to be near him. Nothing had ever felt so right.

Lance sighed and nodded toward the ditch Ash had almost fallen in. "Yuri, what the fuck?"

"Don't ask me. I didn't make them," Yuri said and winced again. He backed up, inching dangerously close to the hole while pressing the palm of his hand to his forehead. Ash reflexively reached out to him, to stop him or yank him back, something. But he sucked in a sharp breath and dropped like a bag of bricks.

"Yuri!"

CHAPTER 25

LANCE CAUGHT HIS BROTHER before he could hit the ground and disappear into one of those ditches that pocked the land in between the trees as far as his sharp eyes could see. He moved his brother a safe distance away and continued to support him. Yuri's legs wouldn't hold his weight.

"What's wrong?" Lance asked.

"My head," Yuri gritted out. He replaced the palm of his hand with his fingers and clawed at his forehead.

"No." Lance bound his brother's arms with one of his to stop him. "This can't be happening."

Lance was ready to lose it. He knew he had to keep it together, but his heart rate sped up like crazy. His heart spasmed in his chest like it had been transformed into a bouncy ball. He could hardly breathe, and he could feel it: he was on the verge of a panic attack.

"I'm taking you home," Lance rasped. He caught Ash's eye and his heart steadied enough to keep him sane. "*We're* taking you home."

"I'm here," Ash said as if to reassure him.

"And then I'm calling Josh," Lance said, hauling his brother up, trying to get him back on his feet. If Ash hadn't touched his hand right then, he probably would've gone into hysterics anyway, but somehow the gesture grounded him. God, what kind of power did Ash have?

He started running at the mouth. "This shouldn't be happening. You were all better. It's almost been an entire month, and you've been all better!"

"I'm okay, Lance," Yuri said, grimacing once again.

"Obviously you're not okay!"

Despite what it may have looked like, Lance wasn't mad at Yuri. He was mad at the universe. He was mad at the fucker who used Black Magic and ruined Yuri's life. It was unfair. His brother didn't deserve it.

Lance and Ash worked together to drag Yuri home. Yuri tried to help, but his legs weren't working. Each step made Lance more worried. It was like Yuri

VALENTINE'S DAY TIGERS

was reverting. He hadn't had a seizure, but this was all too familiar.

When they got back in the house, Lance lifted Yuri up and set him down on their bed. Sweat dripped down Yuri's skin as he took in shuddering breath after shuddering breath. He tried to sit up, but Lance pressed his chest down. "Stay," he growled.

"I'm feeling better," Yuri insisted. "My head doesn't hurt anymore."

"You're not fine, and you're not better." Lance was very close to pulling out his own hair.

Ash stood behind him, warm hand on his waist. "Breathe, Lance," they said. "Breathe."

"I'm going to get Gale," Lance said. "And call Josh."

Lance laid his hand on Yuri's forehead. It did seem like his temperature was back to normal. That was quick—and strange.

"All right, okay, but that's not…" Yuri sighed. "Maybe there's something else we should be worrying about."

"What the fuck is that supposed to mean?" Lance demanded.

"I saw him."

"Him?"

"Luc."

Ash held Lance tighter and pressed their body into his as every muscle in his body tensed. "What? When? Why didn't you say something sooner?"

"I was hoping it wasn't real, but the holes are still there and—"

"Still there?"

"Remember when I dislocated my shoulder?"

Lance crumpled. "For fucking real, Yuri." If Ash hadn't been actively pressing their hand against his chest, massaging the space above his pounding heart, he knew he would have been on the floor, but Ash knew just what to do. Somehow. "Tell me everything."

Yuri said, "I started having some weird nightmares. I figured they were just nightmares, but they were… different, like I was seeing through someone else's eyes. Then I figured out who that someone was: Luc. And I recognized the area he was in. It looked like Eurio with all these black and white spruces. I went out to see if I could find the place I saw in my dream outside of town, and that was when I found those holes, but I convinced myself I was just… I don't know, seeing things, so I didn't bring it up."

"That's not good."

"Yeah."

"So, what's going on exactly?" Ash asked.

VALENTINE'S DAY TIGERS

Lance explained, "When we were kids, we lived on the streets with our dad. He brought us over to the United States from Russia. Looking back on it, I guess he was probably running from something, trying to keep us safe. I don't know. He never said. He just took us and left. We didn't have the easiest time, and our dad got whatever shit jobs he could to keep us fed, but even then we never had anywhere we could stay for long. Then, one day without warning, this psychotic shifter-witch hybrid came and killed our dad. He cursed Yuri with his fucking Black Magic, too."

Ash ran their teeth over their lower lip. "So, there are witches too, and magic… I shouldn't be surprised."

"Turns out the curse is what made Yuri sick all this time. That was why I was never able to help him and couldn't find anyone either. I didn't *know* it was Black Magic making him sick, but a White Witch from this big shifter alliance called Trinity came in over a month ago, and he helped Yuri. He hasn't had a seizure since then, and now he's having nightmares about fucking *Luc Lenoir* himself. We didn't know the fucker's name before, but apparently he's a high-profile criminal as far as Trinity is concerned. This makes everything worse."

"Or better," Yuri said. "What if we catch the fucker

and end this?"

"You aren't going anywhere." Lance poked his brother in the chest when he tried to sit up once again. "Be good, stay in bed, and let Ash watch over you. I'll be back. Ash, don't let him do anything stupid. No setting yourselves on fire."

"We didn't set ourselves on fire," Ash corrected.

Lance threw up his hands in exasperation. "Whatever." He stormed out of the house. He didn't bother with a coat and left a trail of clothes in his wake as he shifted, handing everything over to the white-tiger half of him. Then he ran.

CHAPTER 26

"LANCE REALLY LOVES YOU," Ash said. "He drops everything if it means helping you."

Yuri groaned. "I know. It's ridiculous, isn't it?"

"Maybe it would be if you wouldn't do the same. But you would."

"How do you know that?"

"You're already doing everything you can to make Lance happy. Everything you told me, supporting this thing with me and Lance, telling him not to worry about you. You look out for each other. I've never been close to someone like that. It's sweet."

Yuri snorted. "Well, you are now. Lance picked you. That means everything coming from him."

Ash smiled and looked down at their lap before returning their gaze to Yuri. "You two have a complicated past."

"Kind of."

"Black Magic sounds very dangerous."

"Yeah, it's shitty stuff."

"I grew up in foster home after foster home, without any siblings, without any ties to my past, and I certainly never had anybody to stick up for me the way you and Lance do. I hope you two realize how lucky you are in that aspect."

"I hear you." Yuri looked up at the boring ceiling, following the lines where the different wooden slats met. Yeah, he'd had a lot of health problems thanks to that Black Magic curse, but he knew he was lucky. He wouldn't trade his life for anything. He wouldn't trade his brother for anything either.

"Since I never really had a home, I hit the road with my ukulele as soon as I turned eighteen, and I never looked back. I've never wanted to stay anywhere. I kept traveling, playing music, and searching—though I wasn't sure what I was searching for. Until now. This is the first time I've stayed anywhere more than a week. This is the first time I've wanted to stay. Maybe Lance

VALENTINE'S DAY TIGERS

and you are the family I've been searching for this entire time. I never thought I was looking for family, but I think it must be the truth. There's nothing that feels like this, you know?"

Yuri wasn't sure what to say. He and Lance had lost their dad at a young age, but they had always had each other. He didn't know what it would be like to be completely on his own. He figured he'd be fine after a while, but there was something reassuring about always having Lance there. Even when Yuri felt alone in his sickness, Lance was always there. Then Mateo came along later. And Yuri couldn't forget about Eurio itself. This place had been kind to the twins. This place had become home and extended family.

Yuri and Lance were often closed off, but they were safe in Eurio. Feeling safe didn't come without trust. So, troublemakers they might have been, but those like Gale and Weston saw through them. They cared and kept them here anyway, and they'd help if the brothers asked. Yuri thought of Lance as his one security in life, but maybe there was more security than he thought. He had a safe foundation here that he could always return to.

That was oddly comforting.

"Lance used to be really guarded around me," Ash

said. "These last few days have been a big break-through, but even before that, he was slowly softening around the edges. When I first met him, when I spilled that drink on him, that was probably the worst introduction ever. He got pretty pissed off, but I insisted on helping him out. I got him a new shirt too, before he headed out into the cold. I guess that left an impression on him because I saw him at the bar again one night. He watched me sing. I wasn't sure he'd talk to me, but he was there, so I made the first move again—sans spilling a drink all over him."

Ash laughed. "I'm not going to lie. I thought he was hot as hell. I don't know what I was hoping to get out of talking to him, though. I just did it, and it turned into something. We became friends, exchanging stories, snippets of our lives, though we never got into anything too personal at first. Eventually, I learned about you and how hard Lance was working to help you. I started liking him more and more, not just because I thought he was hot, because of this connection I've never had to anyone. I've had my fair share of one-night stands, but Lance wasn't like that. Isn't like that.

"You know, he was actually the one to ask me on our first official date. We went swing dancing. It surprised me. I had mentioned I loved dancing only once

VALENTINE'S DAY TIGERS

and he remembered. Of course I said yes. It was a lot of fun. He must've had fun too, because he asked me on another date after that. It went on like that, and I started asking him out too. We made loose plans like this or we'd meet up by chance because we never exchanged phone numbers or addresses. We'd touch base at Tipsy or the library, but I think that proves how much we went out of our way to see each other even though both of us were reluctant to give more. Not even reluctant, I think. Just scared."

Well, if Yuri wasn't sure about how Ash and Lance felt about each other before, he was now. Talk about sappy. Gag.

"Dinners," Ash said. "Movies. We'd hold hands, gaze into each other's eyes, and he'd give me this beautiful smile he wouldn't give anyone else. It was all a first for me, and, God, did it feel amazing. I felt loved, but I refused to use that word at the time. It seemed too desperate. Maybe too hopeful?"

"And you felt all that without sex," Yuri said.

"Yeah. I was so starved for all the things Lance gave me that I didn't ask. It wasn't until you showed up a few days ago and we conquered fire that I had sex for the first time in months. And I only did it because I thought Lance was done with me. He'd never been

232

away so long."

"You wouldn't have come with me if he hadn't disappeared on you."

"You're right. I wouldn't have. And I felt guilty when Lance came back the next day. It sort of felt like I had betrayed him? And he knew. I didn't know it at first, but he knew. He came back, apologizing for leaving me so long and without saying a word. He was intent on making it up to me, and we had sex. I thought everything was perfect at last. It was going exactly how I wanted it to. It was like that night I had spent with you put everything back on track somehow. I know Lance is who I want more than anything. That's still true. Lance was worried about telling me his truth, but he had no reason to be."

"Good. Lance needs you."

"You say that like you're not planning on sticking around, Yuri."

Yuri thought about sitting up again, but each time he tried, he got dizzy.

"Do you always put your feelings last?" Ash asked.

"I think you mean first." Yuri smirked.

Ash shook their head. "Does it make you feel lonely, like you're missing out on something? Do you feel like I'm stealing your brother away?"

VALENTINE'S DAY TIGERS

"No. I'm not a sap like Lance. In fact, we're apparently the exact opposite when it comes to romance and sex."

"Maybe, but you're the same in one way: you're both afraid of losing each other."

"I'm not."

Ash raised an eyebrow at him like they didn't believe him. "You both depend on each other more than anyone. It's been like that all your life, and now I've come along to crash the party." Ash cracked a hopeful smile. It was questioning, like they were wondering if they even had the right to smile. "But I feel like I belong here."

"You do. I've never seen Lance so happy. I used to think he would always need me, but I don't think that's true anymore. So yeah, things are changing, but if it makes him happy, it's okay."

"He's always going to need you, Yuri."

Yuri wondered if that was true.

"It's too bad Lance can't seem to appreciate how good you are in bed," Yuri commented, trying to shift the conversation away from him.

Ash was silent for a moment. "Yeah, it kind of is. When Lance and I had sex, I really enjoyed it. I don't think he enjoyed it much at all. It's going to take some time to figure out, but I want to.

"Lance loves me. I don't doubt that, and that means much more to me than sex. He still holds me, takes my hand, kisses me. Maybe it's unusual to keep it at nothing more than that, but that doesn't matter. What works for us is not the rest of the world's business. And you're both *tigers*. You shared a big secret with me, and I don't want to give this up for anything. I think I'll want to travel and sing with my ukulele still, but I want this place to be my home, the place I come back to. Maybe Lance will hit the road with me. Did you know he's a good singer?"

Ash was rambling. Yuri chuckled. "I had no idea."

"I guess what I'm really saying is I want to keep fighting for Lance. Whatever that means, even if it's running across a frozen lake and braving a fire, I want this family."

Another pain shot through Yuri's head before he could reply, and he grimaced. He heard a voice: "*Who is this?*"

"Yuri?" Ash said.

A chill crawled up Yuri's spine, and he bared his teeth. Lance needed to get back here soon.

CHAPTER 27

"IT SOUNDS LIKE TERROS Sight," Cedar finally said after grilling Yuri on everything that had been happening. "To me, anyway. I guess. Maybe Josh didn't neutralize all the Black Magic in your system. Maybe it's connecting you to Luc somehow. You're an Earth Shifter, so accessing Terros, Earth Magic, is possible for you." She frowned and made a call, in which she made a bunch of snappy demands. After she hung up, she said, "Lance, I need to use your computer. My phone can cast to it, right?"

"Yeah, should be able to." He was too tired to ask why, and he was happy to do anything if it would help Yuri. He led Cedar to the living room to get her set up.

Josh was indisposed, so his help was out of the question. He was the only one who ever came close to curing Yuri, so things couldn't get much worse in Lance's opinion.

Lance got Cedar logged on and left her to it. He scrubbed a hand down his face as he went back to his and Yuri's bedroom. Ash took his hand. Gale, Ike, Mateo, and Austin were in the room too. Weston and Cary would have come if Gale and Cedar hadn't said they had this covered.

"Get better," Ike said as he rocked against the bed.

"How are you feeling?" Gale asked.

Yuri was sitting up, so that was a good sign.

"Fine other than at random times and moments it's like I have double vision or something," Yuri said. "'Terros Sight,' according to Cedar. No more seizures, though."

Cedar was alone in the living room, but Lance could hear her voice. She was getting loud again, saying, "It's an emergency. Hell, even the Earth Alpha herself."

"I feel fine now," Yuri said. "Honest." He got off the bed. Lance had half a mind to keep him there, but Yuri rushed past, and they all congregated in the living room.

VALENTINE'S DAY TIGERS

"Earth Alpha," Cedar said suddenly. She bowed a little, her disposition changing as she offered her submission.

Lance glanced at the phone in Cedar's hand, displaying some live-chat app using video, then to the wide computer screen, curious about what the Earth Alpha looked like. The Celestial Alphas were supposed to be among the most powerful shifters on the planet— if not the most powerful—according to Iris and Cedar. This one didn't look like anything special, though. She was small and skinny, delicate like a flower, but then Lance saw something in her eyes that stopped him cold. He had to avert his gaze.

"Let me speak to Yuri," the Earth Alpha said. Her voice was as gentle as a spring breeze. "I'm going to give him a condensed lesson on Terros Sight."

Yuri bent down beside Cedar and took her phone. While the Earth Alpha was clearly visible on the computer screen, voice sounding through the speakers Lance set up, the thing had no webcam or mic of its own. "Yuri here."

"Nice to meet you, Yuri. My name is Rei."

"Trinity's Earth Alpha."

"Yes. For the safety of everyone around you, I'm going to need you to listen closely and concentrate. If

Luc is in the area, as seems to be the case, Eurio could be in danger. Do *not* engage if you have any choice. I'm going to instruct you on how to activate Terros Sight so you'll hopefully be able to track his movements again, consciously this time. If you see him, memorize the location. I will be traveling to you shortly, whether we get concrete information on Luc or not, but the top priority here is for you all to stay safe. I want you to stay in your houses if possible. The only reason you should leave is if you are warning other residents of the danger or if you have a safe place where you can all gather. Understood?"

"Yeah. Got it," Yuri said.

Lance gripped Ash's hand tighter. The Earth Alpha herself was coming to Eurio? That sounded like way too big of a deal. It made him nervous. A cold sweat broke out across his skin. Ash took his other hand and said, "It's going to be okay. We have each other, and we're going to make it okay."

Lance wasn't sure how Ash could say that with so much conviction, especially since they had more reason than anyone to doubt the power of family, friendship, lovers, or anything like that. They said they loved Lance, and they were here after learning Lance was a shifter. They were still here even after Lance had

VALENTINE'S DAY TIGERS

admitted his asexuality.

Ash was all in.

Totally.

Truly.

Completely.

In.

"I'm glad you stayed," Lance said.

Ash bumped their arm into his. "I'll stay as long as you'll have me."

"Then prepare for forever."

"I like the sound of that."

Lance searched Ash's eyes for the lie, but it wasn't there. Ash was truth.

"Me too," Lance whispered.

He ran his fingers along Ash's jaw like no one was watching. No one really was; they were listening to the Earth Alpha just like Yuri was. The touch alone seemed to make Ash's scent sweeten.

Lance dropped his hand, feeling guilty for arousing them like this when he was such a failure as a sexual partner. He wondered what he could do about that. With Ash, he was pretty sure he could learn to be okay with sex. It wasn't that sex was out of the question for him—when it came to Ash specifically. If sex made Ash glow like last time, he thought he could do it and like it for maybe an entirely different reason.

Was that what Ash wanted? He knew Ash and Yuri had their own rather intense physical reactions to each other, but neither of them seemed interested in exploring that again—which he found hard to understand. Why would Ash be so set on him when his brother was clearly the better sexual partner?

Lance looked at his brother, who was now sitting cross-legged in front of the computer screen with the phone propped up against it so it could still capture his face without anyone holding it.

"Concentrate and visualize the space outside of yourself," the Earth Alpha said. They sounded kind of like meditation instructions, something Yuri had never wanted to try in his life. He was either doing something that caught his interest, or he was sleeping. Sitting and doing nothing was not his thing. But he was doing that now, and he was awake. Lance didn't like watching, though. Yuri was only ever this motionless when he was sick in bed. At least his breaths were coming in deep and long rather than shallow and labored.

"If I'm correct, activating Terros Sight will take you directly to Luc because your subconscious is honed in on him after all these years of being somewhat connected to him. Follow that but go back to your body—

VALENTINE'S DAY TIGERS

hurry back—if you feel anything weird. Since you've already been doing this without realizing it, it should be more of the same, but I must promote caution since Bruiser had a bad experience with a Black Witch not so long ago.

"Some witches can sense your spirit outside of your body, this invisible specter, and attack it. This witch put Bruiser into a coma for a few days. We were able to resuscitate him, but only after that witch was killed. Normally, killing the witch responsible for a 'curse' is the easiest, and sometimes only, way to lift it. I would like to avoid something like that again."

"Uh, no shit," Lance said. He broke away from Ash and went to his brother, hands on his shoulders. "Forget Terros Sight. We know where the holes are. That's all you need, Rei. You should be able to pick up the monster's trail there."

"Hands off," Yuri growled, but he kept his eyes closed. "I'm doing it. My choice."

After a moment of silence, Lance reluctantly stepped back. It wasn't because Yuri had asked him to. It was because there was suddenly this empty space where his brother sat, even though Yuri was physically there. When Lance touched Yuri's shoulder again, his body was warm, but *he* wasn't in there. It was an empty shell, a body functioning to keep itself alive, but it wouldn't move.

Lance shuddered as he listened to the smooth breaths Yuri's body took. The room was quiet as death aside from the soft hum of the working computer. Rei sat patiently, her expression neutral on the monitor. Everyone waited with bated breath, and Lance tried not to choke.

Lance counted down the minutes as he brushed against Ash to keep himself steady. Each passing minute Yuri stayed away made him clench his jaw just a little more. He was starting to feel like a windup toy that would break if it was wound back one more rotation. "Come back, Yuri," he whispered.

Lance almost died when Yuri opened his eyes like he had been there the whole time and was just ignoring everyone.

"He's leaving," Yuri said.

"Right now?" Rei asked.

"He has what he came for."

"What is it?"

"It looks like a bone, a big-ass bone. And it feels... wrong." Goosebumps spread all over Yuri's body, and Lance slid down onto his knees to sit beside his brother. He didn't touch him, since he looked so pissed

VALENTINE'S DAY TIGERS

off, but he was close if Yuri needed him.

"I'm on my way," Rei said. "Stay inside like I told you to, and do not face Luc Lenoir. Let him go. You remember the place you saw him, right?"

"Yes," Yuri replied.

"Good. Maybe the energy from this bone will leave a more permanent trail than what we've found in the past." The Earth Alpha frowned. "I'll have Trinity Shifters on standby for calls in case of trouble, but do *not* get in his way."

With how many times she told them to stay put, Lance was inclined to do just that.

Rei shut off the call, and Yuri stood. "I'm leaving," he said.

Lance stood up beside him. "No, you're not. You heard what that alpha chick said."

"That's why I'm leaving. This is bad, Lance. You didn't feel the power coming off that thing. I did."

"So, what? Leave it. What are you going to do about it? His Black Magic is still inside of you and that's why you were able to see him, right? What if you go out there and face him and he breaks you for good?" Lance shook his head. "You can't. You can't face him. It seems like he doesn't realize you're watching him, right? Let's keep it that way. You can't die on me, Yuri. I won't let you."

When Yuri turned to leave anyway, Lance grabbed him. Yuri didn't miss a beat. He spun around and punched Lance square in the jaw. Lance's head snapped back violently, but he held on.

"Let me go." Yuri growled low in his throat.

"Punch me again. See what happens," Lance goaded.

"Stop," Mateo said. His eyes flashed yellow. The wolf shifter had probably been growling for a while, but Lance had been too preoccupied to notice. Mateo's shoulders were hunched over, his teeth were long, and he was about to shift.

"Mateo," Austin said softly as he rubbed his mate's back, "now is really not a good time."

"Okay, everyone, calm down," Gale said. Something red-hot rippled through the air, the alpha in him maybe. This kind of heavy repression wasn't a normal thing that Lance had experienced, but it seemed to call to everyone to some degree, even the untamable Mateo. They all buckled and turned their eyes to Gale.

Yuri tried to pry Lance's fingers off his arm, but Lance held fast. They fought harder than anyone else to resist Gale's alpha aura.

"He's leaving!" Lance said through gnashing teeth.

VALENTINE'S DAY TIGERS

"Why challenge him when he's leaving?"

"We don't know what he's going to do on his way out," Yuri said. "He's going to do something with that bone. It's filled with Black Magic. It feels like a bomb just waiting to go off. What if he destroys all of Eurio before he leaves? He's in the area, way too close to everyone. Look, I know I'm a royal pain in the ass and you all get tired of me, but you're my family. I've lived in Eurio for ten years. If there's one place I can call home, it's this place. I'm not going to let this bastard hurt any of you."

Lance was stunned, stunned enough that Yuri was able to jerk out of his grasp. Yuri shifted in record time, the sounds of bones snapping and reshaping hardly registered in Lance's ears as Yuri went for the window and broke out of it—since the front door was blocked. The shattered glass was an explosion in Lance's ears. Everyone was frozen for a couple precious seconds, and then there was chaos.

Lance shifted and followed his brother out the window. He worried about Ash, but he hoped they would stay put and safe. He just wanted everyone safe.

CHAPTER 28

AFTER DONNING THEIR BOOTS and coat, Ash ran as fast as they could. They were well behind the shifters because they were in animal form. Ash didn't expect Lance to stop for them, and he didn't. If anything, Lance would've wanted them to stay home, but Ash couldn't, not with all the chaos. Ash didn't know if they'd be able to do anything to help, but they needed to do something. This Black Magic made Yuri sick for so long, and it was back. Ash couldn't stand seeing Lance so upset. They couldn't imagine Yuri bedridden. It wasn't right. Ash had found their family, and they wouldn't let this Black Magic take that away.

It was hard to know where the others went once

VALENTINE'S DAY TIGERS

the white and black spruces grew dense around Ash. It was almost as dark out as when Ash had trailed Yuri. At least Ash was prepared this time. Their phone was charged, so they whipped it out and turned on the flashlight. They continued moving as quickly as they could while following the trampled trail taken by several other shifters.

Well, not everyone was ahead of Ash it seemed. Feet pounded snow behind Ash, and Ash looked over their shoulder to see Austin. He fixed his glasses and ran a little faster to catch up. The polar bear cub named Ike was with him too.

"Stay with me, Ike," Austin said. "I know you can run faster than I can, but listen to your teacher."

Ike let out a little grunt, but he stayed close to the man's side. Soon they were all running together.

"We probably shouldn't be doing this at all," Austin said when things had gone silent. "We'll just get in the way." Deep worry lines creased his forehead.

"But we couldn't stay behind," Ash said.

"Well, this all happened pretty suddenly, and you heard how they were talking in there." Austin swallowed hard, his throat bobbing with the effort. "I don't want Mateo to die."

"Yeah, we're doing the exact opposite of what that

Earth Alpha told us to." Ash conceded, and they slowed to a stop. "Let's think about this for a minute."

Austin almost toppled over, but he stopped too, the polar bear cub at his side. "Think about it?" Austin asked. "They're getting farther away."

"If they do fight, we'll end up getting in the way, right? It's obvious to me we don't have anything on the shifters. We can't even keep up, so how are we going to protect ourselves against Black Magic? I don't even really know what that is. What if they get hurt protecting us?"

Ash didn't like this one bit, but they could see the difference. Running had cleared their head and brought logic back into the picture. Ash was left in the dust almost immediately. They were pretty athletic and quite in shape, but the physical difference between them and the shifters was insurmountable.

Austin opened his mouth, but nothing came out. The little polar bear cub grunted, rolled round in the snow, and then jerked up, his head pointing in a specific direction. He let out more little grunts and grabbed at Austin's pant leg with black claws.

"What's wrong, Ike?" Austin asked.

The cub pointed with his paw at Ash—or behind Ash. Ash looked over their shoulder. A sinister growl

VALENTINE'S DAY TIGERS

came from the trees. There was a pair of glowing blue eyes. Gleaming white teeth dug into a huge piece of dark metal, scratching against it hard enough to produce sparks. It was shaped like a bone.

Ash shone their light on the biggest wolf they had ever seen, and the monster leaped into the air like a streak of liquid silver.

Yuri's skin prickled, causing his fur to stick up like the needles on a cactus. He heard the growl. He knew where Luc was.

He turned on a dime, back legs smashing into the snow and through to the ground as he jumped back. He sailed over Lance's head as Lance tried to break into a stop but failed to find traction in the snow. Yuri moved faster, backtracking and evading the deep holes he had reached and dodging the shifters who had come after him. They didn't listen. He didn't want them here, but he couldn't think about that now. He bounded into the heavy darkness cast by trees.

Ash, Austin, and Ike stood in a small snowy clearing. Ash looked over their shoulder the same moment a *big* silver wolf appeared in the air. Yuri made a quick jump, setting him and the wolf on a crash course. He smashed into the wolf with teeth bared and claws extended. At least Luc's teeth were out of the fight because of the huge-ass bone he was grinding his teeth against. It let out metallic shrieks that had Yuri's ears twitching, but he stayed focused.

They grappled in the air, clawing (and in Yuri's case biting) at whatever they could before they both toppled into a mess of flailing limbs on the ground. The wolf smacked Yuri's side with the bone, and Yuri crumpled to the ground. How much did that thing weigh? Luc was on top of him for one second, but Yuri managed to kick him off before he decided to drop the bone and crush Yuri's skull. Yuri couldn't afford to get grounded.

Yuri's heart pounded against his rib cage as he sauntered to the side, slowly circling the monster wolf, sidestepping one way and then the other. The wolf stood, but otherwise stayed where he had landed. That crescent shape flickered on his forehead like a dying lightbulb; it was fatter, almost a half-circle, compared to the last time Yuri had seen it.

At least Ash, Austin, and Ike were safe behind Yuri, and he intended to keep it that way. He sized up the wolf, well aware that he was at least twice Yuri's

VALENTINE'S DAY TIGERS

size. Yuri had never met a wolf that big. But this wasn't just any wolf. It was Luc Lenoir.

Luc foamed at the mouth. Spittle dripped down the ends of the bone in his mouth and landed with a hot hiss in the snow. His eyes dimmed to an almost lifeless gray, and then they flickered blue again. He still wasn't moving, but these little details were wild like a Berserker. Yuri had never stared one down like this. He had never felt this trickle of fear, this cold drop of dread continuously pounding in his stomach. The last time he had felt anything like this was when Luc first appeared, when he slaughtered his and Lance's father right in front of their eyes.

Yuri did his best to make himself an impassable wall should Luc charge forward, but thankfully he didn't have to worry about that for too long. The other shifters had caught up. They moved Ash, Austin, and Ike farther back. One look at Luc was all anyone needed to see they were in danger.

But the monster didn't move.

Yuri gave a subtle glance to the side, gauging how far the closest ditch was. This was a precarious battleground. With everyone safely away, Yuri made a wider circle. It was dangerous to be too close to Luc. They all felt it. It was like static electricity raising their fur. They kept taking steps backward like a shifter hive mind. Yuri heard paws slip and earth tumbling, but he didn't look behind him. He had to trust everyone was being wary of the ditch landmines.

The excessive foam forming in Luc's mouth made it look like he had bitten into a cyanide pill. Was he having a stroke or something? But he was *standing*. His fur made random twitching movements like bugs were biting his skin. He winced continuously and jerked his head from side to side while his paws stayed planted in the snow. Was he getting shocked? Responding to the ticking of a clock? Should Yuri move? Luc was like a sitting duck, but no one thought to take advantage of that.

He probably would've been snapping his jaws like a shark had they not been preoccupied with that huge bone. It weighed his head down and extended out a couple feet from either side of his mouth. It was so thick it barely fit into his mouth. His jaws probably ached. The muscles in his mouth trembled. He was biting down so hard he should've left marks in the bone, but each time he tried to bite down harder, a terrible screech and sparks filled the air. He couldn't pierce through it. He couldn't even scratch it. Maybe it wasn't bone at all, but a piece of steel. Either way, it didn't feel

VALENTINE'S DAY TIGERS

right.

Yuri hunched down. His tail flicked back and forth as he prepared to pounce. Everyone behind him mirrored his actions. It looked like he'd be the one leading the charge—despite Lance's warning growls. But then the bone started reacting. Black smoke rose from it like Luc's teeth had suddenly become hot as fire. Sparks of purple zapped the air and bit fur. Yelps followed.

Yuri couldn't afford to wait anymore. He wasn't going to be able to read Luc no matter how long he studied him. He had to make this quick, so he dashed forward.

The first thing he did was dart from side to side to keep Luc's unfocused gaze from locking onto his position. He dove in, scratched at him, and jumped back before Luc could react, but the stupid bone and whatever Black Magic it was exuding let out energy pulses each time he got close. He leaped forward to gouge out Luc's eyes, but energy exploded out from the bone and sent him flying backward. Lance caught him with the side of his body, but then Yuri was off running again.

Yuri just had to get a good hit on Luc's underbelly. He could tear him open and spill his guts, and it had to happen now because the others had snapped out of their daze. They were about to join the fight. Yuri moved, and then Luc moved. He bowed his head like he had decided the bone was too heavy to keep lifted. He growled. It produced such a deep reverberation that the earth seemed to echo his tone, and the ground trembled. The smoke stemming from the bone stopped drifting into the night and fell down in a thick haze that made it impossible to see. Yuri had no idea where he was going.

He put on the breaks and came to a hard stop. He swiveled his head from side to side, but he couldn't see shit. He couldn't smell anything but burnt tar either. He didn't know where anyone was, and that went for those damn holes too. One wrong move could send him down into a ditch. Even his hearing was messed up. It was like someone pressed mute on the TV remote.

Something flickered in the smoke just as Yuri's throat was starting to scratch. Yelps and zaps suddenly exploded in his ears like the volume was set on high. Spots of light appeared, grew, and coalesced, revealing the sky and Luc standing below it as if a spotlight were shining on him.

He set down the bone, gingerly nosed it, and the light exploded. It pushed away all of the smoke in a rush of wind. It passed through Yuri's body like an

VALENTINE'S DAY TIGERS

electrical current, paralyzing him. However, it only lasted a couple seconds.

The smoke was gone.

Luc was in front of Yuri, and an odd barrier seemed to extend from several feet behind him. Yuri could only guess it was a barrier. It was clear like glass, but it rippled when a purplish spark lit up here and there, revealing a dome. Yuri was inside of that dome, and everyone behind him was just outside of it.

He was trapped inside a magical forcefield cage with a bloodthirsty monster.

CHAPTER 29

THE FORCEFIELD BUBBLED AND rippled when someone headbutted it. It was Lance. The forcefield knocked him backward in a spray of snow and dirt, but he rushed at it again and again. The others followed him. Gale, Mateo, none of them could get through. Cedar even stepped forward, paws alight with Sun Magic. She released a controlled explosion, but the ripple just got more intense, and the feedback was worse. Cedar went flying several yards away and crashed into a tree that snapped in half from the force of her body.

Yuri roared. It was as much a call for the others to stop as it was an announcement to Luc that he was dead

VALENTINE'S DAY TIGERS

meat. Yuri was trapped. No one was getting in to help him, but no one would get in to get hurt either. This worked out as well as it could. He would stop Luc here and now. He wouldn't lose. If Luc got past Yuri, everyone else would be in danger, and Yuri wouldn't allow that.

Without the bone to hinder the behemoth, Luc moved. Fast. All the strange twitches in his body seemed to amp up his speed. Yuri tried to dodge, but Luc grazed his flank with spit-covered teeth. Yuri growled and slashed at the monster. Red blood sloshed in white snow, hot and sizzling against the cold.

Luc charged again. He could've had Yuri's throat this time, but he either miscalculated, or Yuri somehow evaded in time, because his teeth went to Yuri's foreleg instead. He latched down on Yuri's paw and snapped his head to the side, yanking Yuri's body like a rag doll. He kept his teeth locked down, or else Yuri would have gone flying. Pain shot through Yuri as his flesh tore deeper with each shake of Luc's massive head. His shoulder was going to get dislocated again.

Yuri yowled in pain and slashed out with his other paw, barely able to fight against the momentum. He got a good cut across the wolf's cheek, but Luc didn't seem to feel the pain. Red became the prominent color on the ground as Yuri slashed again. This time he narrowly missed Luc's eye, but Luc had had enough. He threw Yuri down, cracking Yuri's back against cold earth, and grounded him. Yuri couldn't even swipe his paws up to rip out the monster's throat. He was bound by powerful legs and paws. The last thing he would hear was Lance trying over and over to break into the barrier, his roars echoing across the land.

But then a voice pierced through his skull, painfully, like a screwdriver drilling its way in. *"Enough."*

Yuri's eyes snapped open. He vaguely recognized that voice. The wolf hovering above him stared intently at him, fighting through the strange tics causing his fur to twitch to keep eye contact with him.

"Find me again when the time is right, tiger."

The pain in Yuri's skull got worse. The pressure built until he was screaming with the pain, and then it ceased as quickly as it had come. When he was able to open his eyes again, Yuri's vision slowly went from blurry to clear. There was nothing weighing him down.

Luc was gone.

The bone was gone.

Yuri was alone in the snow with nothing but clear skies above him. A green aurora moved through it like a meandering river.

VALENTINE'S DAY TIGERS

Dazed, Yuri slowly turned to his side, and shifters surrounded him. Lance protectively hovered over him by stepping one paw over his body to keep him shielded underneath. Lance growled and warned the others back. Then he shifted. As the sound of bones re-forming filled the air, Yuri took in the scenery and realized that everything outside of where the barrier had once stood was blown over. Some trees had even been uprooted. Dirt and big rocks were on top of the snow. It was an entirely different landscape. The holes had been covered up, too. It explained why everyone around him was covered in dirt, he supposed. Some of them were bleeding too, but none of the wounds looked deadly.

"Yuri," Lance said. "Yuri, are you okay?" He touched a lump on Yuri's head. Yuri flinched and roared, opening his mouth wide to show his teeth in displeasure. Lance roared back, and although he was in his human form, it held the same power behind it. Yuri shifted too, realizing communication was in order. It made him aware of just how many cuts he'd gotten as the shift made them worse by opening them wider. When he was finished, Lance's hands went to the welt on his head again.

"Stop," Yuri growled. He batted Lance's hand

away.

Ash knelt down next to the brothers. Thankfully, they didn't reach out with hands all over Yuri like Lance.

"Goddamnit," Lance said. Then he had his arms so tight around Yuri that Yuri could hardly breathe.

"Everyone okay?" Yuri wheezed.

After also shifting back to his human form, Gale replied, "Nothing life-threatening."

"Good. Did anyone see where Luc went?"

"No. It was like a tornado formed outside of that Black Magic barrier. It stopped almost as quickly as it came on. Everything was a mess. Luc was gone and so was the bone. All we saw was you." Gale folded his beefy arms and stifled a shiver.

"Let's go to the Lodge," Yuri said. "Luc gave me a message."

"Great." Gale sighed. He shifted back into his polar bear and gathered his mate and cub. Cedar had a limp but looked okay otherwise. He nudged them in the direction of the Lodge and began rounding up the others as well. Mateo looked like he was going to dart for the trees and run for miles, but Austin wrapped his arms around Mateo's neck and held him close for a few minutes until Mateo was calm enough to follow the

VALENTINE'S DAY TIGERS

others.

"Let's go then," Lance said. He grabbed the back of his brother's head, fingers tearing into Yuri's hair, and then he shoved him away and shifted back to his Siberian tiger. He looked at Ash and then at his huge, striped back. Ash got the message easily enough and climbed onto his strong body. They held on to his fur and rubbed their face into his neck, breathing him in.

Yuri shifted back as well, eager to stave off the cold. He wasn't so injured that shifting was out of the question. He didn't have any broken bones or any dislocated joints, so his cuts had to deal with the change again. Even the cuts were surprisingly shallow considering everything. Right now, the cold was the biggest enemy. He followed Lance once he had finished shifting.

Yuri couldn't ignore this anymore. There was no point hiding what Luc said to him because it was real, and it was a problem. After seeing what he saw and all the years he'd suffered, he needed to stop ignoring the signs. Whatever happened to him when he first ran into Luc all those years ago left them connected somehow.

For some reason, Luc had reached out to him. Maybe it wasn't on purpose but... he knew it meant he had a job to do.

CHAPTER 30

APPARENTLY, TRINITY WAS developing its very own live-chat and video app called the Portal, which Cedar must have downloaded when they first got this computer. There was only one computer available at the Lodge currently, but at least the internet here was pretty responsive. Also, this computer had a webcam, since Eurio was trying to get more connected to the outside world. Some of the new shifters Trinity brought in recently had family overseas too, so this kind of connection was priceless to them.

Yuri sat down next to Cedar at the Lodge computer after Cedar had called Trinity ahead of time for a video chat. Everyone was getting cleaned up, and no

VALENTINE'S DAY TIGERS

one was in the talking mood. Somehow, it got quieter. It was like everyone was holding their breath in anticipation.

"I've got it," someone said, voice sounding through the speakers. "Rei filled me in on the situation." The video on the monitor was grainy at first, but it cleared as a guy sat down. Unlike the Earth Alpha, this guy *looked* alpha. He wore a designer suit that flaunted his physique and deep pockets.

"Samson." Cedar's eyebrows rose.

He sat tall in his seat like a king and raised his chin just a little higher. "How can I help you?" His eyes shimmered a warm brown. "Rei and Jasper are on their way. You haven't run into any trouble, I hope."

Yuri scooted Cedar's chair over rather than fidgeting with the computer screen and webcam so he'd be the primary focus. The lady was not light, but Yuri was strong. The chair's feet screeched across the wood, though. Cedar didn't like that. She grumbled something about scratching the floor but otherwise didn't complain.

"Luc is gone," Yuri said, "but he left a message."

Samson crossed his legs and laced his fingers together as he pressed them against his knee. "A message?"

"He told me to 'find' him again when the time is right."

"Why?"

"I don't know, but I faced him." Yuri looked behind him, at everyone in the Lodge. "*We* faced him, and he didn't kill anyone."

Samson's face was impassive. His expression hadn't changed once since he came on, but his eyes flickered, lighting up in a way that almost reminded Yuri of Mateo—or maybe it was Sun Magic. Solsis.

"You were instructed to stay hidden. There should have been no interaction, and yet you forced one."

"I had to," Yuri growled. "I wasn't going to let him hurt anyone."

Cedar stood up to take care of her strained arm with a hot pad. Gale was ready and waiting. Samson's eyes followed her until she was off-screen. "It looks like he already did," Samson said.

"Who are you, anyway?" Yuri asked.

"The Sun Alpha."

"You might try being a bit more respectful," Cedar called.

"Whatever," Yuri said.

Samson chuckled darkly. "You're a bold one, aren't you? You should have been born a Sun Shifter. I

VALENTINE'S DAY TIGERS

would have liked the challenge."

"I want to help. Take me to Trinity, teach me how to contact Luc again or track him down when I choose to or something. I don't know. I bet Rei could teach me a lot more in person than she can over video. So, take me to Trinity HQ or whatever Cedar called it."

Samson tilted his head. "That she could, and it's nice to see you're so willing. With everything going on, and after Rei's assessment, it might be necessary to bring you in whether you want to come or not."

"Yuri," Lance growled. He came forward and gripped the back of Yuri's chair. "What are you talking about? You're going to leave Eurio?"

"Yes."

Lance balked. "You're just… just like that?"

"It's better this way."

"I'm coming to Trinity HQ too, then."

"No." Yuri growled this time. "I don't want you to come."

Lance scowled. "You don't *want* me to come?"

"You heard me. You'll just get in the way. You don't want to leave Eurio anyway. You want to stay here with Ash, so stay and take what you want instead of chasing my tail like you fucking always do. You're not a cub anymore."

Lance clenched his fists. Yuri had hurt him. *Good,* he thought. *That'll make him leave.*

And it did. Yuri knew his brother well. Lance stormed out of the Lodge without another word. Ash gave Yuri a quick glance, and he held their gaze, unwavering. Then, like he had hoped, Ash went after Lance. Lance would be okay because he had Ash. Ash had been thrown into a shitstorm and had taken it all in stride, with the kind of adaptiveness they needed in this kind of life. They could handle this, and they loved Lance enough to make sure of it. They'd stay, and Yuri would go.

Lance told Yuri he was always stuck as his shadow. Well, not anymore. Yuri was setting Lance free.

"That was dramatic," Samson droned.

"When can I come to Trinity?" Yuri asked.

"First tell me more about your encounter with Luc. We can talk Trinity later."

Yuri almost glanced at the door, like he was expecting Lance to come back or something. But he couldn't do it. This needed to be a clean break. Despite what Lance thought, Yuri had depended on Lance just as much as Lance had depended on Yuri. Maybe more. This was better for both of them. He was convinced of

VALENTINE'S DAY TIGERS

that much.

CHAPTER 31

THE CABIN WAS EMPTY without Yuri in it—in a way. Ash was there with Lance, so it was full in another way.

Lance hadn't talked to Yuri in almost a week. An entire week! The twins had had their squabbles before, but it had never lasted this long. Truthfully, Lance had hoped Yuri would return home, come back to his senses and say he didn't want to run off to Trinity after all. With each day that passed, that was looking more and more unlikely. Rei had come and gone, or so Lance had been told. He never went out to see the Earth Alpha, but she gathered whatever information she could, with whoever she brought along with her, and said

VALENTINE'S DAY TIGERS

she'd be back for Yuri after taking care of some business elsewhere.

Ash sat beside Lance on the new couch. They pulled their knees into their chest and leaned into him, head resting on his shoulder. "You need to make up with Yuri before he leaves. Tomorrow is your last chance."

"I'm surprised Weston and Cary haven't kicked him out yet," Lance grumbled.

"Lance."

"I know. I just don't know how to say... goodbye." Lance wrapped his arm around Ash.

"It's not goodbye. Things will be different since you won't be living together anymore, but that doesn't mean you can't stay in touch. Eurio is connected now, right? We have phones and the internet. It's going to be okay."

"I hope so."

"Take it from a person who has traveled all over North America and has stayed in contact with fans all over the world through social media. That's how connected we can be if we want it."

Lance smiled, but it was half-hearted. "It's not the same, though."

"No, it isn't."

Lance held Ash tighter. Then he curled up against them and pressed his nose into their neck. "I'm glad you're still here after everything that happened. I thought for sure you'd get the fuck out and leave all this craziness behind."

"I'm not afraid of a little craziness. Give me some credit, Lance."

"Oh, right. You and Yuri set yourselves on fire for fun."

Ash rolled their eyes, but they smiled. "We didn't set ourselves on fire."

"Keep telling yourself that."

"Ash."

"Yes, Lance?"

"I want to give you everything you need." He meant that. He did.

"You do give me everything I need."

"Do I?" Ash had to be lying. Their attraction wasn't something they could hide from Lance. He smelled their arousal multiple times a day, almost every time he was with them—especially when they were close like this. Ash had a need Lance could fulfill but didn't, and Ash didn't ask for more. He could smell that odd sweet scent right now.

Ash cradled the back of Lance's head, applying

VALENTINE'S DAY TIGERS

pressure to each fingerprint. "Yes. I've never been happier."

"I want to give you more."

"Lance, you don't owe me sex."

"It's not about owing you sex or not. It's like when I take you out on dates. Yeah, I enjoy it too, a lot, but I'm doing it and picking places I think you'll like because I'm so in love with you. I like to see that glow on your face when you've smiled so much you say your cheeks hurt. So, I'm not great at sex, but I'll learn to read you, and I'll learn how to give it to you the way you like it. You don't know how badly I want to please you."

Ash flushed, and their sweet scent grew more intense. "Keep talking like that, and I'll explode." Ash interlaced their fingers behind Lance's neck. "If *you* want to try sex with me again, I won't say no."

Lance smirked. "I know you won't. I can smell your need."

Ash's face burned hotter, and Lance kissed them, long and slow. Ash was uncharacteristically shy. They had kissed too many times to count, and Ash was holding back. They started holding back ever since Lance admitted sex was not his favorite thing. He doubted it ever would be, but he liked this much less. He didn't

272

want Ash to feel like they were overstepping any time they wanted to kiss him deeper or any time they got aroused and pulled back because they didn't trust themself to stop. Lance had observed all of it this last week, and it wasn't what he wanted.

He was deeply moved by how much Ash cared for him and the fact that they stayed after everything. If Ash was willing to be so considerate of him, Lance wanted to reciprocate. And he had time to think about it. He much preferred Ash glowing to not having sex. He was pretty sure he'd do anything to see Ash happy. He wanted that smile permanent on their beautiful face to match their rainbow hair.

To prove his point, Lance breached Ash's teeth with his tongue. Ash was happy to let him in, but they hesitated with initiating anything more. So, Lance took the lead again, catching Ash's tongue with his. That broke part of the cautious barrier Ash had erected. They held Lance tighter, dug in deeper. Ash kissed him like they'd never get to kiss him again. And it was him. All him. Ash meant every word they had said to Lance. Yuri was just a couple miles away, but Ash wasn't staying for Yuri. They were staying for Lance. They chose Lance.

VALENTINE'S DAY TIGERS

This felt too good. Lance was on top of Ash, kissing them, muscles flexing. He hadn't pinned them like this before, and Ash liked it. They liked it a lot. They held his neck and kissed him deeper as their bodies pressed together on the couch. Ash was good and wet, but they didn't know if Lance was hard yet. Or if he wanted to be.

"What do you want to do?" Ash whispered against Lance's lips. They were breathless together from the intense kisses alone. Ash's lips were almost numb, but a warm buzzing undercurrent set their body on fire.

"What are you in the mood for?" he asked.

"Everything or anything. Handjob, blowjob, straight sex, whatever you want."

Lance hummed. "Nope. It's whatever *you're* feeling, babe. Tell me what you want."

"More kisses."

Lance smirked. "That's easy."

Ash introduced their teeth, hoping Lance would get the message. He did. He bit back, turning this kiss into something rough, something so hot Ash was already turned on high. They couldn't stop the moans that escaped their lips and the way their hips rolled up, seeking something to sate this need. Ash hit Lance just right and moaned again.

Breathless, Ash said, "I've never felt like this with anyone."

"Is that good or bad?" Lance asked.

"Good. Very good." Ash ran a hand down Lance's side to his hip. They rolled up his shirt and buried their fingers inside the band of his jeans and briefs so they could touch his skin "If you don't want me to touch you anywhere, just tell me, okay?"

"Okay."

"Do you have any condoms?"

"Yep. In that drawer. Yuri bought a new supply. May as well use them so he can't take them to fucking Washington or wherever Trinity HQ is."

"Vindictive." Ash cupped Lance's cheeks. "Tomorrow you and Yuri are going to make up. When we see him off, if you two haven't made up, there will be hell to pay."

"And what kind of hell can you bring on twin tiger shifters, Ash?"

"Hey, I've mastered fire. You don't want to test me."

"With Yuri's guidance. That's like the apprentice trying to top the master when you have much less experience. You're doomed to fail."

VALENTINE'S DAY TIGERS

"You never know. Maybe I'm more naturally talented."

Lance laughed. "Sure."

"I'm serious, though. Tomorrow, before Yuri leaves—"

"I heard you." Lance kissed Ash again, bringing the heat back tenfold.

Ash snaked their hand forward, grabbing in between Lance's legs. He jolted at their touch and bit back a groan. He was half-hard. When Lance didn't pull away or tell Ash to stop, they unbuttoned his jeans by feeling alone. He stayed hovering over them, watching Ash's face while they worked. When Ash had Lance's length in hand, they gave him a quick rubdown and watched as his body tensed. He was good and hard now, physically ready for Ash. Ash's thighs trembled with need.

"I think I want it straight," Ash said. "Any second thoughts?"

"None," Lance replied. He got off the couch and scooped Ash up into his arms. He moved rooms and carefully set Ash down on the bed he and Yuri would no longer share and kissed Ash's forehead as if they were as delicate as a flower.

Ash sat up and got undressed after Lance did the

same and went to the nightstand to grab a condom. Ash lay back against the pillows and spread their legs wide. Their body throbbed, and they were tempted to touch, to coax that explosive ecstasy, but they waited, and Lance arrived quickly. He crawled in between Ash's legs. Ash loved seeing his skin on full display like this. The sight of him alone made Ash's heart and sex throb in unison.

"Do you want me on top?" he asked.

"Yes, please." Ash was addicted to having Lance on top of them. With Yuri, they hadn't liked it. He was too wild, too powerful, and Ash needed to take back some control, but Lance… Lance could always be on top. Ash surrendered everything to him. Only him.

Lance was thinking too much, though. Ash could tell. He was meticulous about getting the positioning just right, not sure when to thrust or if he should at all.

"Hey."

Lance met Ash's gaze.

"Breathe. Even if we don't have 'perfect' sex ever, it doesn't matter. You're with me, and that's all I care about."

Ash moved, sitting up and forcing Lance to do the same. They weren't sure if he'd like this or not, but they thought they'd give it a shot anyway. They got on all

VALENTINE'S DAY TIGERS

fours and placed their hands on Lance's thighs as he sat back on his legs. Ash kissed his neck, starting from the center and moving all the way to his left earlobe, which they took into their mouth.

"Fuck," Lance breathed.

"Is that a good fuck or a make-it-stop fuck?" Ash asked.

"Can it be both?"

Ash leaned back and laughed. "Yes, it can be both. You can say no, by the way. There's never a point in *this* when you can't back out. You know that, right?"

"You keep reminding me, so I'm not sure how I couldn't. I'm still with you if that's what you're trying to ask."

Ash sat on his lap. They spread their legs out to either side, resting their knees on the bed and their ass on top of Lance's powerful thighs. Lance spread his legs a little wider, and Ash rolled their hips forward. Ash held Lance's back tightly as they rolled their hips again. Lance was so hard, so ready. Physically. Was he ready emotionally?

"Ash."

Ash's eyes fluttered open. They hadn't realized they had been closed. They stopped rolling their hips, but their body quivered a protest. "Lance."

"Shifters usually have a way of claiming a mate, and even if we aren't the type to instinctively stick to one partner, it's often a mark that can be left for each coupling. Most bears like Cedar and Gale bite their partner. Cedar and Gale are permanent partners, mates for life, though, so they might renew that bite or keep it at one bite, depending on their needs. It's kind of... weird. Wolves are naturally inclined to one life partner and males have this instinct to bite their females, I guess. It combines scents more permanently than having sex without the bite. Basically, shifters like to stake an extra claim, total domination and possession."

"Do you want to bite me, Lance?"

"Well, not really." He shrugged. "And big cats tend to go crazy with their claws." He held out his hand in between them, flexing his fingers. Then he pressed his palm flat against Ash's chest, right over their heart. "I guess... I just want you to know that it doesn't mean I don't want you as permanently as the others want their mates. I do."

"I don't doubt your love for me, silly tiger."

"Good because I don't know how to tell you how much I love you. I don't know how to show you either. I think this might be a start, though."

VALENTINE'S DAY TIGERS

It was. The fact that Lance was willing to try sex again for Ash, because it made Ash happy, meant a lot to them. It showed just how serious Lance was about wanting to give them everything.

Ash rolled their hips forward. Their sex throbbed, and they really needed to come. They needed Lance now more than ever, all this talk about love, having him so close, it was agonizing not to be closer. "Take me," Ash begged. "Please."

Ash rose up high on their knees, and Lance took the cue. He grabbed his dick, positioning himself for Ash, and Ash came back down. They didn't allow their body to acclimate to Lance's size. They were wet enough for more than adequate lubrication and took him as far as he would go. Ash's entire body shuddered, and a deep groan consumed their throat.

"Hard. Fast." Ash could barely get out the words.

"Not the easiest position for me to do that." Lance growled and caught Ash's hips. Then he moved them both with ease. He grabbed Ash's ass and kept their bodies pressed together as he somehow laid Ash down on their back. And then he did what they wanted. He thrust hard and fast. Ash gasped and clawed at his back while begging for more, while crying his name. Each time Lance moved, Ash bucked their hips up to meet him. Ash knew they'd feel this tomorrow, but they didn't care. Ash screamed when they came. Lance wasn't very vocal, but he let out a deep moan when Ash's body massaged his, coaxing him to hit his climax as well.

Lance huffed and dropped, barely holding himself up enough not to crush Ash underneath him. Sweat glistened on his skin, veins bulged blue and prominent, highlighting the stark contrast between natural white skin and the dark black of his tattoos. Ash couldn't help but stare, because he was beautiful. Just beautiful.

"How was it this time?" Ash asked.

"It wasn't completely terrible last time," Lance clarified. "I just knew I didn't feel it as deeply as you did. It was like you had some kind of revelation, like sex was what you had been anticipating getting from me, and it wasn't the same for me." He held himself up with one arm and used his free hand to grab Ash's waist. He rolled them both onto their sides while staying buried inside of Ash. Ash wasn't in a hurry to let him go and wrapped their top leg around his, pressing their foot into the back of his thigh. Last time, Lance had pulled out immediately, like he couldn't get away soon enough.

"This time was better, though" Lance informed.

VALENTINE'S DAY TIGERS

"But I'm ready to tear off this condom and take a shower."

Ash spit out a laugh. "Will you wash my hair?"

"Uh, hell yeah."

"And then hold me all night?"

"Definitely."

"Then let's go, handsome." Ash touched Lance's face and kissed his lips. "Thank you."

CHAPTER 32

H E STILL WASN'T HERE.
Ash had been on the lookout for Yuri since they had arrived at the Lodge with Lance. The tables had been stowed away to make room for a dance floor. Lights, of the pink and red variety, had also been set up for Valentine's Day. Pink, red, and white hearts decorated the walls, and streamers curled down from the steeply angled ceiling. The place was packed. It seemed like everyone in Eurio was here—except for Yuri. Ash didn't know all of the shifters in Eurio yet, but at this rate, they'd know them all by heart soon enough.

Yuri would be leaving for Trinity HQ in the evening. The Valentine's Day dance was moved up to the

VALENTINE'S DAY TIGERS

daylight hours so that everyone could attend his farewell.

"Did Lance give you those chocolates?" Cedar asked as she danced her way to Lance and Ash with Gale in tow.

"He did. They were delicious. I had no idea he made them! They looked and tasted better than store-bought chocolates." Ash said.

"Thanks to my guidance."

Cedar puffed out her chest, and Gale spun her around to whisper in her ear. "Enough boasting, my love. Everyone knows you're the best chocolatier here."

"You mean I'm the only one."

"That too."

Lance stole Ash away, expertly stepping away in time to the music to once again give them their own little space on the dance floor. He looked damn good in a suit. Ash had never seen him wear one before, but now they only wanted him to wear suits. It hugged his body in all the right places. Plus, they were wearing matching suits, both a velvety red. It let the world know they were a pair.

"I heard Cedar was in charge of brunch too," Ash said.

"Yeah, Cedar just one-upped everyone today," Lance replied. "You can go date her now."

"Sorry, I'm already mated to the best shifter in the world."

"I dropped the ball this time, though. Sorry, Ash. I meant to make plans tonight too, but it just didn't happen."

"This evening is for Yuri. I understand." Lance averted his gaze, but Ash placed a hand on his cheek to capture his eyes again. "I haven't seen him. He is coming, isn't he?"

"He's known for arriving fashionably late or not at all. I think he'll come, though." Lance shook his head. "But enough talk about Yuri. I asked you to dance with me, and we haven't done much dancing." Ash tried to take another sweep of the Lodge with their eyes, but Lance took their chin. "Eyes on me."

There was no need for him to say it twice. Ash was enraptured by him. The closer they got, the stronger Ash's feelings became. Lance showed up in their life one day and changed it. Ash had met a lot of people in their life, but none of them had changed Ash's life the way Lance had. Ash knew they wanted to spend forever with him. Ash was pretty sure they'd go off to travel and sing again from time to time, but for now

VALENTINE'S DAY TIGERS

they were drinking in the novelty of staying in one place. They wanted to stay in Eurio until being there felt normal, like the home Ash had never had.

"Think you'll hit the road with me when I start traveling again?" Ash asked.

"If you'll have me."

"I'll have you everywhere, Lance. Forever and always." Ash tapped his nose. "You know that means you'll have to sing with me too, right?"

"I'll try not to think about that part."

When the current romantic ballad ended, Cedar took the makeshift stage and announced, "And now we'll have a special number performed by Ash with their ukulele."

Ash grabbed the back of Lance's neck to pull him down for a kiss. "It's my time to shine."

"Knock 'em dead, beautiful."

"I feel a little nervous for once. I've never had an audience that has been waiting for me to sing for the last week. I always go to one obscure bar after the other, you know? Fans never knew where I'd be next, so they couldn't catch me. I've never cared about making a good impression at any of these places either because I usually left the next day."

"You've got to be kidding me." Lance grinned. "It'll

be easy, Ash. Let the music take you like it always does. Watch me and nobody else."

"Any day now, lovebirds," Cedar said. Gale stole the mic from her and kissed her soundly in front of *everybody*. Cheers rang out across the Lodge as everyone seemed to egg them on.

"Guess I'll go now," Ash said. When they turned, Lance pushed the small of their back to get them moving faster. A grin found its way onto Ash's lips, and they had the sneaking suspicion that it would remain there for the duration of their performance.

Ash stood at the front of the Lodge, where the makeshift stage had been erected. All eyes were on them. There were no cloudy eyes affected by too much booze. They were all bright and fully attentive.

Ash hadn't lied about the sudden jitters. This was new for them, but it wasn't bad jitters. It meant, for the first time, that Ash cared. It was like a part of them they never knew existed had awakened.

Ash took their ukulele out of its travel case and left the case propped up against the wall. Then they made sure the instrument was tuned.

After clearing their throat, Ash said, "I wrote this song for Lance. It's called 'Something Only Butterflies Know.'"

VALENTINE'S DAY TIGERS

Ash was ready to strum that first chord, to set the key for themselves, but then something caught their eye. Someone just walked in through the front door, blasting the room with natural light, and that someone was Yuri Lenkov. He wasn't dressed up like everyone else. He was wearing jeans, and when he stripped his winter coat, he wore only a simple dark blue sweatshirt underneath. When he caught Ash's eye and gave his signature smirk through a full beard, Ash smiled so wide their cheeks hurt.

Finally, they thought.

The first chord rang out as Ash's fingers started moving on their own, playing from pure muscle memory. Everything faded away but the one person Ash focused on: Lance. The rest of the room dimmed to black as an imaginary spotlight singled him out. That was when Ash's nerves stilled. They sang the first note and the next, and it was all for Lance.

Walking along a road that never ends
A rhythm made by feet on earth
Lyrics and stories stream in my head
A record of all the places I've been
No destination made for me
I am on the road to nothing

KESTRA PINGREE

And I meant to keep it at nothing
But a kaleidoscope of butterflies find me

I have heard it said a time or two
There's something only butterflies know
It's a feeling, a wondrous feeling
It starts in your stomach and grows
No destination made for me
I am on the road to nothing
And I meant to keep it at nothing
But a kaleidoscope of butterflies find me

They fly from above
In a vortex called love
I swallow them whole
Then lose all control

It all starts with a look
A simple look from a stranger
A short exchange of words
There isn't any danger
Your eyes tell a story I've never heard
I hardly know you, but something inside of me stirs
That should be the end
I've recorded your story

VALENTINE'S DAY TIGERS

But I come again
Guided by fluttering wings
Because your eyes tell a story I've never heard
What was cold is now warm, and there is more

That's when I know
I've discovered what only butterflies know

The pink and red lights flooded the entire room again once Ash strummed the final chord and applause filled the air. Everyone in the room moved in two bodies: those who came to Ash and those who went to Lance.

"Your voice is flawless," Cary said.

"Lance is lucky to have you as a mate," Weston agreed. "Cary can't hold a tune for—" She jabbed him in the ribs with her elbow.

"Thank you." Ash grinned and excused themself. They accepted all the nice words that floated their way as they made it to Lance's side. Lance grabbed them around the waist and lifted them into the air like they didn't weigh a thing. Ash laughed and hugged him when Lance set them back down onto the ground.

"You were fantastic," he said and kissed them.

"Thank you," Ash whispered against his lips.

290

"Yuri's here. You know what that means. It's time to set things right."

CHAPTER 33

ASH TOOK LANCE'S HAND without another word and did their best to move him to the other side of the Lodge. Lance dragged his feet. He dragged them even more when he saw Yuri leaning against the wall with his arms folded. He could have stopped and torn away from Ash's grasp, but he needed to face his brother. He looked good. All those cuts had faded considerably. He didn't have a lump on his head anymore either.

Lance missed him.

They had never been separated for so long. They usually fought and had it all out in one go, but this wasn't like every other time. This wasn't even like when Yuri was sick because they had still been to-gether. It turned out death wouldn't be the thing to take Yuri away. Yuri was taking himself away.

It was time to say something.

Ash held fast and dug in their heels when they got Lance in front of Yuri. Lance couldn't find any words. His jaw went slack, and he just took his brother in. He knew his brother like he knew the back of his hand, every tattoo, the color of his eyes down to the little flecks no one ever thinks about when describing some-one's eye color. Yuri was Lance's twin, his other half—or so he thought. Did this mean they had outgrown each other? Was that a thing that could happen to twins?

"Hey," Yuri said as he pushed off the wall. "If you keep staring at me like that, I'm going to lock you in a chokehold until you pass out."

"Asshole."

"There we go."

Lance had a million things he wanted to say, and he couldn't say any of them. So, he didn't. He stepped forward, closing the small space between him and his brother. Yuri stiffened like he was expecting Lance to introduce his fist, but all Lance did was throw his arms around his brother and hug him as tightly as he could.

VALENTINE'S DAY TIGERS

Yuri expelled a rush of air and slapped Lance on the back a few times, sort of acknowledging his hug, but the slapping got more insistent the longer Lance held on.

"Okay. Enough already," Yuri said.

But Lance didn't let go. "God, I'm going to miss you, pain-in-the-ass brother. Will you at least check in once in a while? Once a week? Even once a month?"

"I can probably handle that."

Lance didn't care that everyone was watching. He didn't care about anything other than memorizing his brother's earthy scent all over again and hugging him hard enough to leave an impression of his warmth for years to come.

Lance's eyes burned. God, he was getting sick of that feeling. He was pretty sure he had cried more these last few months than he had in his entire life. He hated it.

"You gonna let me go yet?" Yuri asked.

"Can't get away from me soon enough, huh?"

"It's not like that, Lance."

"Then what is it like? You're suddenly leaving. You've always been impulsive, but this... this is—"

"I finally have some direction. You should be happy."

"I never cared about that. Those are Gale's words."

Yuri grabbed the back of Lance's head and pressed his lips to Lance's ear so only he would hear his next words. "You're going to be fine, Lance. I've seen you with Ash. A day was all it took to see what you mean to each other."

"But what about you?"

"I'm going to be fine, too."

Ash broke out of the almost-crowd surrounding the brothers; everyone was trying to give them some privacy, but it was obvious many were listening. Misty eyes were the most common sight in the Lodge as Ash wrapped their arms as far around both brothers as they could.

"Come back and visit, Yuri," Ash said.

"You'll wish I hadn't. I'll wreck the place."

"Shut up," Lance growled. "You've already wrecked the place. What more could you do?"

Mateo intruded next. He slugged Yuri's arm and asked, "You sure about this?"

"Yeah."

"Good luck, then. Beat Luc's ass next time you see him for all the shit he's done. Break free."

Yuri grinned. "You got it."

"And be careful."

VALENTINE'S DAY TIGERS

Yuri rolled his eyes. "Okay, Austin."

"I told you to cut the shit out before Austin got here."

"Yeah, you and Lance always worried too much."

"You know that's not going to stop."

Austin came over then and hooked his arm around Mateo's waist. "I'm sorry for... well, for anything you felt I had against you. It wasn't that. I just worried about Mateo, and sometimes you three would—"

"Set yourselves on fire?" Ash asked.

"Uhm, no," Lance said. "That's grade-A Yuri right there. Mateo and I always had a little more sense than that."

"Yeah, like the time we broke the generator at the Lodge to sell off the parts to some psycho in Fairbanks," Mateo added.

"What?!" Gale roared. "That was your reason?"

"The guy was weird. I wanted to see what would happen," Yuri said. "He ended up trying to buy the parts off us for pennies, saying it was all he had and that we'd be doing this in the name of art. We gave him the stuff anyway, but I have no idea what the fuck he ended up doing with it. Pretty sure he had a few screws loose, but we got a tour of this shed he kept full of his unconventional junk art in the back of his house."

"Spirits."

"He was nice, though. Gave us hot chocolate and called us kids."

"We were twenty, not that old," Lance reminded. "And Mateo was seventeen."

"Still, not kids." Yuri cocked his head. "You know what's crazy? You six," he pointed out Gale, Cedar, Mateo, Austin, Lance, and Ash, "should form a club."

"Why?" Lance asked.

"Because one after the other you've gotten mates for the holidays. Like, what the fuck is that all about? You're now the Holiday Romance Club."

"Don't like it," Mateo growled.

"It sounds terrible," Austin agreed.

Yuri shrugged.

"Hate to break up this nice little chat after the Cold War has finally ended," Cedar chimed, "but the Earth Alpha and her mate are landing soon. It's time to go, Yuri."

The Valentine's Day activities moved to where the fishing shanty sat along the Tanana River. The cubs who were too young for the dance came too. Then everyone took turns saying their goodbyes. Hugs, an

VALENTINE'S DAY TIGERS

exchange of words, handshakes, there was no shortage of those when it came to the permanent residents at least, members of the Toran Pack and Loike Clan.

They all stood on a wide stretch of flat pebble-pocked land that eventually led into the water. Today, it would be used as a landing site for a helicopter. The helicopter could be heard now, blades spinning rapidly and sending out forceful winds that struck trees and picked up the snow weighing down their branches. Everyone stood safely away from the buffeting wind as the farewell came to an end.

Soon after the helicopter landed, the engine cut out. The remnants of the warbling noise it had made caused Lance's hearing to pulse, but it went away as soon as his attention was drawn to the Earth Alpha. She was tinier than he thought, much shorter than him and even Ash. And yet she, Rei, was one of the Celestial Alphas. Lance didn't know what to make of it.

Another shifter came out right after. He was the exact opposite of Rei. He was positively huge, likely even an inch taller than Gale. He smelled like a bear of some sort.

"It's good to see you again, Yuri," Rei said and held out her delicate hand. It was like a bird's wing.

Yuri accepted her offer and gave one firm shake

before letting go. "Yeah, likewise."

"This is my mate, Jasper." She indicated the bear, who nodded rather than speak. "I hope you have the patience to learn everything you can about Terros Sight. The more you know, the better we'll be able to utilize whatever connection Luc seems to have established with you."

"Yuri and patience?" Lance said. "Good luck with that."

"Hey, for once I'm trying to make a good impression," Yuri said. But he held his hands at the back of his head, elbows extended, and swayed from side to side like he was bored already. Then the helicopter caught his eye and he stalked around it instead.

"That has to fly you miles away. I wouldn't mess with it."

"Lance, stop being such a fucking pill."

"Are you afraid of flying, Yuri?" Rei asked.

"Nope. Haven't done it in years and never in a helicopter, so hopefully it'll be slightly interesting before it gets boring and I sleep the rest of the way there." Lance could practically see his brother's tail twitching. If he had been in his tiger form, it would have been.

"Take care of him," Cedar said. "He can be a handful."

VALENTINE'S DAY TIGERS

"He might be the one to help us break through the Circle. Those Black Witches are connected to Luc, and they've been up to... something. We'll take care of him," Rei said. "Thank you for your willingness to help, Yuri."

"Sure."

"Let's get moving then." Rei signaled the helicopter pilot, and then she went back inside and got seated next to Jasper.

Yuri headed for the helicopter's open door too, but Lance grabbed his wrist. "Make sure you call, video, something."

"I will, okay? I *promise*." Yuri rubbed his knuckles on top of Lance's head, making his nearly white hair stand on end with the generated static electricity.

Lance tried to swallow the lump in his throat, but it stayed. If nothing else, Lance had to say this one last thing. He was certain Yuri already knew it, but he had to say it. "I love you."

"I love you, too," Yuri said, and he didn't tease. "Thanks for always looking out for me. I got better because of you."

"You got better because of Josh."

"Not like that, Lance. You never gave up on me. It wouldn't matter if I was dealing with seizures and

PWD now or not. I'd still be making this choice."

"I know that. The only thing that ever stopped you was the seizures that laid you up. And you're wrong, Yuri. I did try to limit you and stop you from being so reckless even more because… because of a disability. I tried not to, but it was hard sometimes. You never did, though. If you wanted it bad enough, you took it. You never gave up on you."

Yuri grinned and hugged Lance so fiercely he lifted him off the ground. "Yeah, that too. But still. See you later, man."

"Bye, Yuri," Lance managed to reply through squished lungs.

Yuri let Lance go and climbed into the helicopter. He dropped onto his seat and the door closed moments after. Lance kept his eyes locked onto his brother as Yuri glanced out the window. Ash came to stand at Lance's side and took his hand. He squeezed in reply, but he didn't look away from his brother. Lance and Ash took one step backward and then another, until they backed up as far as they had to so the helicopter could take off.

The helicopter's rotor system got to work, sending another barrage of wind to everything around it. Lance shielded his eyes with one hand, and he kept

VALENTINE'S DAY TIGERS

looking. He looked and looked until he couldn't see Yuri anymore and the helicopter disappeared into the quickly darkening sky above.

It felt like a part of him was slowly tearing with the growing distance, but it wouldn't rip off. He stayed together, in one piece, even though the twin who had been half of him, more than half of him, for so long, was leaving.

Lance wasn't a shadow anymore. Maybe he never really was. Maybe the real reason Yuri left was to prove that.

Lance was solid, flesh and bone, and he would be just fine.

EPILOGUE

IT WAS TIME TO video chat with Lance. It'd been a week like Yuri promised, and he missed his brother anyway. It was weird not seeing him every day. But it had also been just fine. There was plenty at Trinity to keep Yuri busy—most of the time. His new teacher was literally everything he could have ever asked for.

Yuri logged on to one of the computers in one of the communal rooms at Trinity HQ. It was a big-ass building with millions of windows, and Yuri had gotten lost in it more times than he could count already, but he was getting the hang of it. Also, this place, Talepeaks, was a shifter-run and owned city. It couldn't be reached by car, and it had strict flight regulations. The

VALENTINE'S DAY TIGERS

security was insane.

This communal room had several little cubicles for privacy, and each one was equipped with a computer, a wide-screen monitor, a webcam, headphones, whatever. It could be used as a work station, for recreation (sort of, Trinity had a strict protocol for just about everything it felt like), graphic designing, programming, and so on. Yuri could still hear others talking outside of his chosen area, but he couldn't make out the words. Privacy.

He opened the Portal in a window and logged on there too. He had a notification from Lance already. Lance was his only contact right now, but he'd probably end up with more eventually. Or not. He wasn't big on communicating this way, but he'd do it for his closest people.

Yuri clicked on the icon of his brother and Ash. *Figures he'd use one of those couple photos,* Yuri mused. Lance was a hopeless romantic, and Yuri had never realized it. No one had. Hell if his brother wasn't good at hiding things, but they'd always fester and get out eventually. That was how Lance worked.

The message Lance left said he was ready when Yuri was. It was sent five minutes ago, the exact time they were supposed to be chatting. Yuri called and enabled video, and Lance picked up a second later.

"Hey!" Lance answered after one ring. He was beaming. He looked better than Yuri had ever seen him. This was Lance at his happiest. His eyes seemed bluer than normal, darker maybe. They were less icy.

Yuri grinned. "Hey yourself."

Ash smashed their cheek against Lance's, smiling with the best of them. "Yuri, how's it going?"

"It's going."

"Fun or boring?" Lance asked.

"Both. If it wasn't for all the shitty Terros Sight training, there'd be plenty of trouble to be had."

"Maybe they're just trying to keep you contained."

Yuri shrugged. "The training is getting somewhere, so who knows. Went through a couple teachers already since Jasper and Rei are busy and important. Now I've got Zoe."

"Is she hot?"

"Hot is an understatement."

"Don't tell me you already slept with her."

Yuri shrugged and a lazy smile rested on his lips. "What can I say? I'm smooth."

"And things aren't weird yet? You have to keep seeing her since she's your teacher, right?"

VALENTINE'S DAY TIGERS

"Well, I nailed her before she was assigned as my teacher. The night I first spent here."

"On Valentine's *Day*?"

"Oh my god." Ash laughed. "That means you're part of the club, Yuri. What did you call it? The Holiday Romance Club!"

"I *fucked* her. She's not my mate, and there's no romance."

"But have you slept with her more than once?" Lance asked.

"Yes."

"New record."

"Whatever. Zoe is cool. I guess we're as much a thing as anyone, but we don't do dinner dates and that shit. Dinner with Zoe turns into a food fight. I think everyone here is getting sick of us. We also have secret conversations all the time whenever there are boring Trinity meetings, so that's nice."

"Secret conversations?"

Yuri signed without speaking. He and Lance hadn't used sign language much since his PWD went the way of the dodo, so Lance was taken by surprise, but he got it.

"Zoe's deaf?"

"Yeah. Also, she's wicked fast. I challenged her to

a race when I was ready to flip my shit with all the sitting around and Terros Sight training. I couldn't figure out what animal she was, so that was the deal. We shift, we race, and I fall on my fucking face."

"You're a real poet, Yuri," Ash said. "It sounds like Zoe was made for you."

"She's fun."

Lance chuckled. "So, what kind of animal is she?"

"A flying squirrel."

Lance's chuckle turned into gasping laughs. "She's absolutely perfect for you."

"How are things for you two?" Yuri asked.

Lance wrapped his arm around his mate and kissed them on the cheek. "Good. I feel like we've figured things out."

Ash smiled softly, and their green eyes shimmered. "Yeah, we're good. Every day I spend with you gets better too. I like knowing you like this, without either of us hiding. It's… it's perfect." Ash kissed Lance on the lips, soft and lingering. Their lips touched lightly, on and off, and Yuri wondered if they planned on going at this for hours.

He rolled his eyes at the disgusting display of affection. He could deal with romance as much as he needed to, but hell if he didn't gag whenever a couple

VALENTINE'S DAY TIGERS

sweet-kissed for too long in a movie or whatever. When he and Zoe kissed, it was foreplay and nothing else. That was how he liked it. Kissing like Ash and Lance did just felt weird to him.

"Have you guys heard about the reporter?" Yuri asked. Finally, the two stopped kissing and took his bait.

"Reporter?" Lance asked.

"Oh, maybe it's a no-no, but whatever, too late to take it back now. I thought Cedar and Gale might have said something about it."

"Spill, Yuri."

"Some chick named Haley Buchanan got shifter footage of some big shot named Cedric Snow."

"I've heard of him," Ash interjected. "He's a shifter?"

"Indeed. Haley's just an amateur human reporter, but she won't let it go. She's got copies of the video in who knows how many places. Trinity's combed the web, but she's smart. She's got physical copies, and likely digital too, stored on her own local devices. Trinity's kind of at a loss. She's demanding to meet with the Celestial Alphas, and they're actually considering it, or they've agreed to it. I don't really know, but it's been one hell of a drama around here. Guess the Celestial

Alphas think they could use this tenacious human on their side."

"What? Wow." Lance raised his eyebrows. "Does this mean shifters are… coming out?"

"Could be."

"God, I hope not. I can't even imagine what that would be like."

"Well, that's sort of Trinity's end goal, you know. They just want to do it in their own time and in their own way. Maybe they think this chick is the beginning of that. C'mon, Lance. It could be fun."

"Or it could be fucking awful."

Ash growled. "Don't worry, babe. I won't let them hurt you."

"I'm stronger than you," Lance said.

"Not anymore. I'm the tiger shifter now, the badass. We've switched roles. Didn't you hear my impressive growl?"

"It was impressive, but it doesn't work like that. You've always been a badass anyway."

"It's about fucking time, though." Yuri cut in. "How many years has it been since this planet began and shifters and humans have been separate like this? That's insane. I'm ready for a change."

"You're always ready for a change."

VALENTINE'S DAY TIGERS

"It's gotta happen someday, just like I'll find Luc eventually. It's better to be adaptable." Yuri tapped his fingers against the desk as a jolt of invisible energy surged through him.

"No updates on him, then," Lance said.

"Not yet, but what he said has been bothering me. I don't know what he's talking about with this, 'Find me when the time is right,' shit, but he picked the wrong shifter to blindly take orders from him."

"Yeah, he did."

"I don't answer to anyone."

Lance growled. "No, you don't."

"If you ever need our help, Yuri, just say the word," Ash said. "We're family. Now that I know what that word means... I just want you to know you can count on me too."

"Thanks, Ash." Yuri grinned.

The conversation returned to simpler things after that, like talk about what the others were up to in Eurio. Mateo and Austin were finally going to have that wedding Austin had been asking for, and Yuri was supposed to fly out to Eurio to celebrate with them all. He figured he could handle that. He was happy for Mateo. For Austin too. Weddings didn't mean much to him or Mateo, as far as he knew, but it meant a lot to

Austin.

Yuri continued listening with a contentedness, knowing that everyone was, well, happy. The feeling that bigger changes were ahead rested just underneath his skin in the form of barely contained energy, but he was ready. He was a fighter, he didn't take anything lying down, and he was alive.

What do you think of Trinity? This shifter world has many more books coming. Why not check out *Her Brave Wolf* next? Marked by the Moon is the series Bruiser was first introduced in. All Trinity series have crossovers, so look for familiar faces!

BOOKS BY KESTRA PINGREE

Marked by the Moon
Her True Wolf
Her Brave Wolf
Her Fierce Wolf
Her Wild Wolf
Her Noble Owl
Her Bad Cat

The Lost Princess of Howling Sky
Phantom Fangs
Taken by Werewolves
Saving the Werewolves
Queen of Werewolves

The Holiday Shifter Mates
Halloween Werewolf
Christmas Polar Bear
Valentine's Day Tigers

These Immortal Vows
Demon Snare
Angel Asylum
Desire

Guardian

On the Precipice

The Soul Seer Saga

The Wandering Empath

The Lonely King

The Lost Souls

The Beautifully Cursed

The Lunar Dancer

Novels

Blind to Love

NEWSLETTER

Never miss a new release by signing up for Kestra's newsletter.

kestrapingree.com/subscribe

MESSAGE FROM THE AUTHOR

Thank you for reading *Valentine's Day Tigers*.

If you enjoyed the ride, please consider leaving a review. Tell your friends too. If you're anything like me, you're already shouting your favorite stories from the rooftops. I commend you.

Your support is what allows me, and so many wonderful authors, to write these stories for you, so thank you.

From the bottom of my heart, thank you.

ABOUT THE AUTHOR

Kestra Pingree is a creative who doesn't know how to stop. They are first and foremost a writer and storyteller with an endless library of books in their head just waiting to be typed. They are also an artist and animator, as well as a singer, songwriter, and voice actor. One day they swear they're going to make their own video game, too.

If it involves creating, they are there.

They can also be seen cuddling their cat, reading, or playing video games.

kestrapingree.com

Made in the USA
Coppell, TX
07 March 2020

16374667R00185